Return

to

Sandpiper Cottage

W. M. ANDREWS

ೞഔ

Sparrow Ink
www.sparrowink.com

ISBN - 978-1-989634-45-5

www.wendymayandrews.com

Stay in touch with Wendy May Andrews
and forthcoming publishing news.

Sign up for her biweekly newsletter

She had to lose everything to figure out what *truly* mattered...

Rachel Whitney is lost. Alone. She needs a place to heal and figure out where her life went wrong. Where *she* went wrong. But the emotional—and financial—scars her late husband inflicted on her complicate *everything*. Now, her only sanctuary is the *last* place she ever wanted to see again.

Sandpiper Cottage.

She's not surprised to find the house her aunt left her in disrepair. It's also just her luck that the only available handyman was once the boy who let his friends torment her in high school.

She can now confidently say her misery is complete.

But the good thing about rock bottom is that there's only one place left to go. And it's not long before she realizes it *is* possible to build a beautiful life for herself—maybe even a life that includes a second chance at love.

The only real question now is if that life will be at Sandpiper Cottage, or somewhere else?

Return to Sandpiper Cottage is an angsty but wholesome and enchanting Contemporary Women's Fiction novel. Readers of all ages and backgrounds will love the empowering message at its heart.

This women's friendship fiction book will bring you all the feels. If you love women's fiction with a side of clean romance, this is a great fit for you.

Dedication

This book is by no means biographical, but I did lose my own dear aunt two years ago. The grief and guilt that Rachel feels mourning for her aunt were inspired by my own losses. I know that mourning and grief are complicated but the old adage about wounds and time is true. I dedicate this book to all those dealing with loss and I wish you a happy ending as Rachel finds. In the meantime, I hope some time escaping into a book will do you some good.

Acknowledgements

My first acknowledgment has to be of my own dear aunt who helped inspire my love for books.

Next, my awesome, supportive husband. Without his easy-going nature and technical assistance, my books would never make it to publication.

My beta team – Monique, Alfred, Suzanne, and Christina – are the first to ever lay their eyes on each book and give me invaluable feedback. Your assistance is always appreciated, thanks for being on my team!

Editors are every author's most important partners and I am blessed with two – Bev Katz Rosenbaum and Julie Sherwood. If you find any mistakes in this book, those are entirely the author's fault.

My gorgeous cover is thanks to Les at GermanCreative.

Chapter One

"You didn't come this far to only come this far." *Big breath in, slow breath out.* "Things don't happen to me; they happen for me." *Big breath in, slow breath out.* "Tough times don't last; tough people do." *Big breath in, slow breath out.* "I am capable. I am strong. I believe in myself." *Big breath in.*

The slow breath out stuttered on a small laugh stretching Rachel's lips. She wasn't sure there were enough motivational mantras she could possibly murmur to get her through this moment.

The brief bit of humor helped her not throw up as the ferry chugged closer to the island she had sworn never to return to. Her nerves steadied slightly, but her stomach still churned. It wouldn't be so bad if Aunt Eileen was going to be there to greet her. Of course, if Aunt Eileen was still there, this would be an entirely different situation. Her dear aunt would have come to her in Rachel's time of need, rather than Rachel coming to the island.

Dear Aunt Eileen would never again be there to greet her, though. The deep tide of grief threatened to suck her back into its grip, but Rachel had cried enough in the last weeks to last her a lifetime, and she refused to do so now.

Despite her previous vow to never return to the Cape, Rachel was now seeing it as almost a refuge after the terrible debacle that was the last six months of her life. She could rebuild a new life for herself in the safe cocoon of her childhood home.

Or maybe not her childhood home. Was teenhood a word? She'd have to Google it.

In either case, despite her misgivings about returning to Cape Avalon, it had really been the only decision open to her. And it solved at least a couple of her problems, even if it created a few more. But that didn't change the tightness in her neck and shoulders and the queasy pit in her stomach at the thought of returning.

"Return to your vehicles. We will be disembarking momentarily." It was the third time the announcement had sounded. She really ought to follow the directions.

Digging deep, Rachel tried hard to be positive. Really, no sane person would consider it a bad thing to be inheriting a free house on an island not that far from civilization. Of course, inheritance meant someone had died. In her case, her last living relative. The aunt who had taken her in when her parents had been killed in a car crash when she was thirteen. So once again, she was on her way to Sandpiper Cottage after losing someone in tragic circumstances. In this case, again, it was two tragic losses. Back-to-back.

And Todd's death *was* a tragedy, she insisted to herself. Anyone's death was. The fact that his death had confirmed to her that she had never really known him, and he wasn't the man she had thought he would be when they married didn't change the fact that dying at the age of thirty-five is beyond tragic. No one, not even a man who lies to his wife about his spending habits, should die so young. She needed to ignore the relief that pulsed through her whenever she realized she would never again have to hear his insults that were couched in seeming concern for her feelings. The so-called endearment "Honey" was forever ruined for her. She needed to ignore the relief because guilt always quickly followed.

Surely it couldn't be right to be relieved by one's husband's death. Of course, the fact that she hadn't been implicated in his accident that didn't seem to be an accident was a huge relief. The police were still investigating but they had ruled her out as a suspect. Rachel might never know what really happened to him, and she didn't feel she needed to know. He probably had owed money to the wrong people. She was just lucky they hadn't come after her.

The fact that Aunt Eileen's cancer took her before she could see that Rachel was finally free to move on with her life brought on the threat of more tears, so Rachel turned her face into the wind and let it brush away her worries at least for the moment.

A deep, cleansing breath reminded her that it was always a surprise that the ocean air didn't smell salty. Despite her complicated feelings about the island, she had always loved the freshness of the air. Even if it did unmentionable things to her hair, she added to herself as she reached a hand up to grab the locks that were threatening to obscure her view of the rapidly approaching island.

The ferry would be docking soon. It was well past time for her to go down to her car. But she hadn't prepared for the sense of anticipation that flooded through her and never would have expected. She thought she was dreading her return and she was, she insisted to herself. But clearly a part of her was excited about it, too.

Fresh starts had always excited her. Even the ones that had been forced upon her. She'd had plenty of those. This one was no different. The fact that it involved Aunt Eileen, even though she had already passed, seemed fitting. Her aunt would be thrilled if she knew how much of a load the bequest of Sandpiper Cottage was taking off her mind.

Even though Rachel had promised herself she would never return to the island, it suddenly felt like a hiding place from all that had gone wrong in her life in the last decade. If it didn't turn out to be the sanctuary she hoped it would be, it would at least allow her to catch her breath for a moment without having to worry about having a roof over her head.

The thought of living in a box under the overpass did not appeal to her in the least, especially not with winter approaching. A slight shudder made its way through her in the company of a fierce gust of wind as the ferry made its way out of the more protected channel onto the open waters where it was to dock at the very end of the island. Rachel had never properly understood why they didn't make a straight run from mainland to island instead of going to the end as they do, but she wasn't really a city planner so what did she know?

Shaking her head with a sigh, Rachel finally turned away from the rapidly approaching dock and started on her way down to her car, surprised to note she was the last left on deck. Since it wasn't tourist season, she supposed everyone else was tired of or immune to the view. Since she hadn't come to visit since she had left for college the day after her high school graduation just before her seventeenth birthday, she supposed she had an excuse for not being immune to the beautiful view.

Avalon Cape was beautiful in any season. And even if one had their reasons for hating their experience on the island, it was undeniable that the island itself was a gem.

She only hoped she wouldn't have to see a single person she had previously known.

That was a ridiculous and futile wish, she was well aware. With the way the land leases were set up, they rarely passed out of families. That was the only reason she was actually there at that time. If she didn't take up residency that week, she would lose Sandpiper Cottage within the next couple of weeks, since Aunt Eileen had died six months ago, almost to the day. Rachel would have to live there for at least six months in order to keep the lease. If she couldn't fulfill the lease requirements, she'd have to sell the house her aunt had loved so much. Most people spread out their six months throughout the year if they weren't year-round residents. But since Aunt Eileen had died six months ago, Rachel would have to stay a full six months in a row in order to have the lease transferred into her name as her aunt had stipulated in her will. Aunt Eileen wanted Rachel to have all that she had possessed. And Rachel wanted to fulfill that wish for her aunt.

A wave of guilt whipped through her. She hadn't even returned to the island then. Her stomach clenched as she remembered why. Todd had insisted she attend some stupid work conference with him. In hindsight, she should have recognized how ridiculous it was that he wanted her to attend with him. But hindsight was always a much clearer view than anything in the moment ever was. At the time she had felt like she was underwater in the situation.

And so, she had not attended her beloved aunt's memorial service. She had arranged it all, of course. But she hadn't attended. Shame would be her constant companion over that one.

Just as she arrived at her car, Rachel squared her shoulders. Aunt Eileen would have understood why she didn't attend. She would also be glad that Rachel was finally free of Todd and on the road to recovering her sense of self.

She didn't even know who Rachel Whitney was anymore. And that was what she hoped to figure out in the time she spent on the island.

Part of her hoped to keep Sandpiper Cottage, but she didn't know if she would be able to fulfill the residency requirement. Even these next six months on the island were going to be a strain. But it would give her the time she needed to figure things out.

And perhaps learn to live with all the various sources of shame she had collected in the past nearly two decades.

Ok, Rachel, you're being ridiculous. It had only been fifteen years since she had stormed away from Avalon High School, vowing she would never set foot on island soil after the disaster of her graduation ceremony. No need to add more than necessary to the intervening years.

Even though she felt like an old lady, she knew she would be considered in her prime at thirty-three years of age. It was only the worries that had etched themselves onto her face. Now that the worries were gone, and if she could stop crying every other minute, with the help of the facial cream the woman at the store had insisted she invest in, Rachel was nearly certain she would be able to look her age, regardless of whether or not she felt haggard and ancient.

Living with grief since the age of thirteen was probably what made her feel like a crone. That and the choices she had made along the way.

But the moment she drove off the ferry she was starting fresh. And there was no room for all these negative thoughts in her fresh new future, Rachel reminded herself as she slid her finger along her phone, unlocking it so she could resume the mantras playing over the Bluetooth in her small car. She nearly snorted. They hadn't worked yet but surely one of these times. Hope continued to spring from somewhere deep within her.

Chapter Two

One of the multitude of worries that dogged Rachel had been whether or not she would be able to find the cottage after all this time. She had very mixed feelings when it came into view. Relief to be near the end of her journey and that her dying car had made the long drive was high on her list of emotions. But seeing the condition of the house had her heart sinking. Whatever she planned to do with Sandpiper Cottage, it was obvious it was going to need a little bit of TLC before she could either comfortably live there or sell it for any kind of profit.

How had Aunt Eileen let it get that way? She had always prided herself on keeping it in top shape.

Guilt again threatened to swamp Rachel, but she bit back the prickle of tears that threatened behind her eyelids. Crying now was only going to make it worse.

Obviously, Eileen had been weaker than she had let on for longer than she admitted, Rachel acknowledged as she stared up at the still beautiful beach-side house in which she had spent her teen years. Any property so close to the ocean faced constant wear and tear. It was one of the costs of being at the beach, she supposed.

Even the dock seemed to have washed away. At first, Rachel couldn't even see where it had been, but a more careful study of the beach let her see the remnants of what had once been the dock and pier they had happily lazed on during the long summers on the island. Now all that was left resembled an eerie skeleton.

Aunt Eileen's home was at the furthest end of the island, almost on the corner. So, the dock was somewhat protected from the worst of storms and weather, but it still took a hammering whenever bad weather came through. It had never been in the very best of shape from what Rachel could remember, but it had always been there. Her heart broke just a little bit more as she stared at the evidence of her own neglect.

She really ought to have come in person to check on her aunt at some point in the past decade, never mind that Todd had never wanted her to, and Eileen had seemed more than willing to come to them. Rachel knew she shouldn't have accepted her aunt's word that everything was fine, especially after she had finally admitted to Rachel that she had been diagnosed with cancer.

If Rachel had known it was terminal, she would like to think she would have come, but really how could she know since she had never come for any other reason? With a shake of her head to dislodge her inertia, Rachel climbed out of her car, grateful to at least have a roof over her head.

And no matter the baggage she might be carrying with her, no one could remain completely wrapped up in their problems when they had the beautiful Atlantic Ocean just outside their front door.

It had always been that way for her. Even as a grieving thirteen-year-old, staring at the never-ending waves that lapped at the shore was soothing to her.

And she was counting on that steady presence to help her regain her feet after all her recent losses. Surely, if she could survive the loss of both her parents at the age of thirteen these recent troubles wouldn't be the ones to break her. And she had Sandpiper Cottage to root and ground her, even if she no longer had Aunt Eileen.

"Hellooo!"

Rachel cringed. She wasn't ready for anyone friendly. But she couldn't shame her aunt by being surly. She turned toward the sound and tried to smile.

"Welcome to the island. You must be Rachel. Your aunt talked about you all the time, and I've seen pictures, of course, but it's a delight to meet you, even if it's at such a terrible time. I'm sorry for your loss. I suppose I ought to say your losses. I've never known of someone to have so much tragedy as you."

Rachel stared at the woman who seemed to have no filter, wondering how to respond. Thankfully, it didn't appear as though a response was expected as the woman just kept right on talking.

"Did you drive all the way today? No, of course you didn't, no one could drive all that way by themselves in one shot, could they? I've been keeping an eye out for the place, but I didn't have your number, so I couldn't have really told you even if something was to happen, could I? But I knew you'd come along eventually. And then, of course, Eileen's lawyer stopped by last week to tell me you were on your way, so I've been keeping an eye out for you. I guessed it would be today. Wasn't that lucky?"

Rachel blinked when the woman finally fell silent as though awaiting a reply. Which question was she to respond to, she wondered?

"Thank you for keeping an eye out, that was neighborly of you," she finally said with a tight smile.

"Bless your heart, you don't know who I am, do you?" the woman pronounced, suddenly sounding far more southern than Rachel would have expected to hear on the island. And the expression made her sound like a little old lady rather than barely much older than Rachel herself from the looks of her. Rachel tried to bolster her weak smile but wasn't sure if she managed it.

"Your aunt talked about you so much that I expected she probably was doing the same about everyone around here to you. I'm Evelyn Wright. I moved in about seven years ago. Your aunt and I became fast friends."

"Ah yes, please forgive my rattled brain. Aunt Eileen has mentioned you from time to time," Rachel finally squeaked out. She didn't add that she had envisioned someone far different from her aunt's descriptions. From the few things Eileen had said, Rachel had pictured a much larger, more frazzled looking woman, not the perfectly put together little creature that was grinning up at her. She supposed it was the force of the other woman's personality that made Rachel think she would be bigger than she was. It was hard to imagine all that energy contained in such a small package.

"Of course, my dear. All that driving. You must be fair to falling asleep on your feet." With those words, Rachel felt as though the woman was actually herding her toward the house much like a collie would with a flock of sheep. "I put a casserole in the oven for you on low to stay warm as I had no way of knowing what time you'd arrive, and I was only guessing that it would be today anyway. I know your aunt mentioned you have had some strange eating habits in the past, but no one can resist my casseroles. You just go on in, have a bite and get yourself a good sleep.

11

Everything will be perfectly right and tight in the morning."

Rachel wasn't sure if anything would be right for her ever again, but she accepted the other woman's words for the kindness they were meant to be and made good her escape, grateful that she had grabbed her overnight bag before being ushered into her house. Everything else could wait.

Evelyn's casserole smelled heavenly. The scent of warm garlic wafted from the house as Rachel opened the door and dropped her bag in the foyer. She hadn't eaten all day, not wanting to waste what little money she had left on the expensive food on offer at the interstate stops. Rachel had barely noticed that she was hungry but suddenly her stomach was growling as though she hadn't been fed in days.

It was true that she tried a lot of diets in her adult life. It didn't take a shrink to tell Rachel they were all in a bid to control something about her life. But in that moment, she couldn't even remember which fad she was supposed to be following, all she wanted to do was devour whatever was in the oven.

Control was something she valued highly, though, and she managed to not eat directly from the oven dish. Instead, she portioned out an acceptable serving onto a small plate and took it into the front sunroom where she could watch the crashing surf in the light of the setting sun. A few minutes later, stomach finally full, Rachel was able to look around at the beloved house she had inherited.

She had made the right decision despite her long-ago vow. Nothing Cape Avalon contained could hurt her worse than the last fifteen years had done. And it was surely going to be better than worse.

Just as she had feared, though, it wasn't just the dock that was showing signs of decline. Looking beyond the layers of dust that had accumulated in the six months since Eileen's death, Rachel could see that there had been no updates done to the house since she had left the day after graduation. It didn't even look like a great deal of routine maintenance had been done.

Poking around, Rachel found a small bag of tools in a closet. She was certain that she would be able to figure out most of it with the help of some videos online. A part of her was actually looking forward to the attempt. It was time for her to start her new life. Repairs to the house were a good, almost symbolic, place to start.

Chapter Three

*A*n odd little duck that one seems to be, Evelyn thought as she wandered back to her own house. Certainly didn't have any of her aunt's chattiness, that was for certain. Look how much talking I had to do just to cover over the awkward silences. With a shake of her head and a glance back at Eileen's once beautiful home, Evelyn shrugged to dismiss the worry she felt forming for her late friend's niece. Heaven knew Evelyn had enough problems of her own to deal with; she shouldn't be taking on the cares of some self-centered young woman who couldn't be bothered to visit her only living relative until after she had died.

Evelyn tried to smooth out the frown she could feel creasing her forehead as she stepped through her own door but wandered toward a window that would allow her to continue to look over at Sandpiper Cottage. She wasn't so old, she needn't make herself look it through worrying.

Eileen Whitney had been well ensconced in their small community on this side of the island when Evelyn and her husband had moved into it. But she had kindly opened her door and her heart to her new neighbor. Evelyn had sensed that the other woman had needed someone to dote over since her niece never came to visit, and Evelyn couldn't really be too much older than Rachel, even though she felt to be about one hundred. She supposed that's what the cancer and then the fertility treatments did to you. And all the worries and cares that came along with them.

Shoving the unwelcome thoughts from her mind with determination, Evelyn continued to speculate about the newest arrival to their lane. She supposed she would have to help the other woman out. She was certain the other women on their street wouldn't do it. Too wrapped up in their families and their careers to take much note of their neighbors, those ones were. It would fall to Evelyn.

Except her husband wouldn't like it much. Not that Eric would notice. Especially not if she was careful. Like the casserole. Evelyn made sure to cook one for them too so that any smells would be accounted for. Not that he would be home in time to notice the smells or maybe even taste the casserole, what with him burying himself in work. But he so liked to worry about her. Well, perhaps liked to worry wasn't the right way to put it, no one liked to worry. But he did it very well. Evelyn tried not to give him more reason than the obvious ones that couldn't be avoided. He just couldn't understand that doting on others was her way of relaxing. He should, though, considering he did the same thing in his own way.

With a sigh and a twitch, Evelyn moved her curtains into place blocking out her view of her neighbors and keeping her personal worries inside for herself to be concerned with. If the neighbors thought she lived a charmed life, she would allow them to do so. And really, she was grateful to be alive and Eric did his best, she knew he did. But he had wanted children nearly as much as she did. Losing that dream, along with the fear of losing her, had done strange things to both of them. Her therapist said they would be able to get back to each other one day.

She just wished that day would hurry up and get there.

But perhaps helping her new neighbor settle in would make the time pass faster. In either case, Evelyn was willing, determined even, to find out.

Chapter Four

T he fresh new day dawned just as it always did at Sandpiper Cottage. The air was so fresh. Rachel felt more rested than she had been since she left fifteen years before, taking deep, lung-filling breaths of the sea laden air. She had always attributed her exhaustion to her heavy workload at school or work and all the responsibilities that were heaped upon her shoulders.

But in that moment as she stretched and yawned and sat up in bed she knew, deep in her soul, that her exhaustion had been the sea missing. Her heart sank at the early reminder that she had been a fool.

Rachel refused to accept such a negative thought so early on her first day back. Thoughts like that certainly weren't going to help her fresh start. She was where she needed to be, and it was going to work out this time. Surely a competent, well-educated, supposedly intelligent woman of thirty-three could figure out this thing called life.

First thing she did, before she even got out of bed, was grab her laptop. The writing coach whose book she'd just read insisted that setting up habits needed to be established first thing. Her morning coffee would be her reward after she wrote for at least twenty minutes. And Rachel was certain that the sense of accomplishment would set her day on the exact right course. Everything else she needed to do would follow.

If only her life was as easy to control as that of her characters.

Rachel shoved the negative thought away from her mind. She was determined to create a happy, light story for readers to enjoy. Any negative thoughts were not to be entertained until she had gotten in her goal word count for the day. And even then, she ought to ward them off as best she could.

If she was going to become a bestselling author of feel-good stories, she needed to feel good herself. That was what the mindfulness groups she was a part of were all about.

She couldn't help but smile, even if it was in twisted amusement with herself. She really was in a lot of online groups. Perhaps she would get more writing done if she spent less time online.

But then she sank into the world of her characters and everything else was able to drift away for a time. Rachel was pleased with her progress when the beep of her timer coincided with the growling of her stomach, and she closed her laptop after carefully saving her document. She had read horror stories of authors losing all their work from improper storage practices.

Todd had told her countless times she couldn't succeed as an historical fiction author, something she'd dreamed of for years, but Rachel was trying very hard not to believe him. It was a challenge, though. As a forensic accountant, numbers were her thing, or rather they had been. Rachel was taking a sabbatical to try to recover her bearings after recent events. There was nothing creative about that. Well, perhaps there was if looked at from one perspective. Some of her former clients had certainly been creative in how they had kept track of their numbers.

A yawn stretched her jaw while she stretched her arms to work the kinks out of her shoulders as she made her way to the sun-filled kitchen and started making her breakfast. For the briefest moment she missed her old job. But she didn't trust her accounting abilities anymore. What kind of an accountant didn't notice that her husband was spending all their money and racking up huge amounts of debt?

Part of her reason for coming to the Cape was to hide from the shame. Her boss had tried to tell her it didn't matter, but Rachel's confidence was rattled, and she didn't feel she had the fortitude to stand up to clients as she once had. Maybe after she took her "little sabbatical" as her boss had called it. Rachel wasn't sure if she would ever want to return now that she had learned that the control she had always thought the numbers gave her had all been an illusion.

Realizing she was allowing her thoughts to derail her day, Rachel quickly spread a little peanut butter on a slice of bread she had toasted after she knocked off the ice that had accumulated on it after who knew how long in the small freezer over the fridge. She would definitely need to hit up a grocery store that day. But first she needed to shake off her negative energy with a brisk walk along the beach.

She firmly believed there wasn't a single problem that couldn't be dealt with successfully with a bit of time spent walking on sand, listening to the ceaseless waves. Rachel should have remembered that when she graduated instead of her rash vow to never return. Nothing felt that simple, though, when you were about to turn seventeen. The passage of time had allowed Rachel to forgive herself for that error in judgment.

Now she just had to work on forgiving herself for the rest of her history.

Staring out at the surf, Rachel thought she might need a few years of therapy to accomplish that rather than the six months of beach time she had allotted herself.

But it would at least be a good start. And hopefully she'd have her finished novel to show for it. Or maybe several. She had started many manuscripts that were now in various stages of progress. But every time she had been excited about one project or another, Todd had managed to slip in the necessary amount of doubt for her to put that project aside, never to return to it. Whenever the urge to write had surged within her, she had always started a new project. Case in point, the one she had been fiercely working on ever since Todd's untimely death.

Rachel was determined to find her backbone somewhere here along the shore. Where she had lost it so many years before. Then she would be able to get on with her life as a successful adult whether that was as an adult accountant or as a grown-up novelist. She would accept either case as long as it was her choice and not something she allowed to happen due to the circumstances she put herself into.

And that was what she blamed herself for. Well. Herself and Jake Callaghan. But she certainly wasn't ready to think about him. She had never asked but she assumed he had left the island like nearly every other young person did. Rachel was far from prepared to face him. Perhaps a few more years of that therapy she kept meaning to sign up for would allow for that. She smiled over the sarcastic thought. Already the beach was doing her some good if she could find some sort of amusement in her high school memories.

She kept her eyes averted from the carcass of the old dock. It was much too heart-breaking and somehow symbolized her losses.

Even though she was hiding here as a refuge from the shame and sadness of her marriage and the failures of her life, Rachel was determined that her time at Sandpiper Cottage, whether temporary or permanent, was going to result in her facing her future and settling her past. She was going to rebuild her life into one about which she could be proud. Or she'd die trying, she supposed, but that was a blacker thought than could be borne on such a lovely day. With a nod of determination, she set off back toward the house. It was time to tackle it one project at a time.

Hours later, Rachel wasn't certain if she had chosen wisely. She had reasoned that since dust settles, she ought to start at the top of the house in her cleaning frenzy. And frenzy it had been. She ached in every muscle she knew about and new ones she had never thought of before. She was filthy and hungry and ready for bed once more. And she still hadn't stocked the kitchen as she had intended to do.

Despite feeling like she could sleep for a week, a glance at the clock assured Rachel that the day wasn't so very advanced. She would have time to clean up and get to the store before it was time to cook supper. Of course, the growling in her stomach let her know that she had skipped lunch, so supper would be welcome any moment.

After a quick shower, Rachel decided she would reheat a little of Evelyn's casserole before she set out for the small village. She was an adult, who was there to say what time her meals needed to be? She could count that as her evening meal and be done with it. Whatever she bought at the store would be provisions for the coming days. She could be a more responsible eater soon. Or she could claim she was fasting. That was always fashionable.

Debating between whether or not she needed to put makeup on, Rachel assured herself she didn't know anyone and there was nobody she was trying to impress, so she went without.

And regretted that decision as soon as she pulled into the parking lot.

"Is that you, Rachel?"

The gleeful exclamation made Rachel want to slink into the floorboards of her car. Someone recognized her, and she hadn't bothered with her appearance. Rachel did her best to climb out of the car with dignity or at least not fall on her face and embarrass herself further.

"Tina, how are you? I didn't expect to see you."

Tina laughed and waved away Rachel's surprise. "Of course, you didn't. You haven't changed a bit," she declared. "How have you managed to stay frozen in time? I swear I've gained ten pounds for every year that has passed since we have last seen each other."

Rachel blinked and searched for a reply. She had never known how to answer such a rejoinder. Ought she to deny it? While she didn't have a scale on her and doubted the other woman had actually gained a hundred and fifty pounds, she certainly hadn't stayed the slim cheerleader she had been when they'd known each other before.

"You still look great, Tina," Rachel said with sincerity. It was true, despite the extra weight, the woman still looked pretty and stylish, unlike how Rachel felt. "Are you just visiting or have you moved back?"

"Did Eileen not tell you?"

Rachel nearly groaned over the question. Aunt Eileen had not been a gossiper. She had spent their conversations expressing her concern over Rachel's situation, not telling her about her friends and neighbors. She just kept her eyebrows lifted and hoped the woman would elaborate or disappear.

"We've been back for six years now. Can you believe it? We were in such a hurry to get out of here once upon a time, but now we're all trickling back. Even you, it would seem. Who'd have thought?"

Rachel's determination to be polite nearly evaporated at those words. She had been forced into coming back. She hadn't had some epiphany and suddenly thought Cape Avalon was her dream destination. But she would do whatever she had to not to be homeless. Not that she had anything against the homeless, she just didn't want to count herself amongst them.

"Well, there you go," she finally managed to mumble as a non-answer. "It was nice running into you." She was proud of herself that she had managed to say that last lie with a straight face. She couldn't very well tell the woman she wanted to throw up at the sight of her. But that's how she felt as she regretted the delicious helping of Evelyn's casserole she had treated herself to before setting out to the Pick and Pack.

"I hope we'll be able to see a little more of each other if you stick around," Tina called after her, but Rachel pretended not to hear. She hated to be rude, but she also had no illusions about being friends with the former cheerleader.

Tina might not have been a part of the group who had tormented her in high school, but they hadn't been really friends either. Rachel didn't have friends back then or now. Life with Todd had made that difficult even if she hadn't had her challenges as a youth.

Having moved at the age of thirteen and then later being one or two years younger than everyone else in her class in high school had meant making friends was difficult, so she hadn't stayed in touch with anyone she had grown up with. She was always envious of people she heard of who were still best friends with people they had gone to grade school with. Would her life be any different if she had friends like that? How would her life be different if she had *any* friends?

She hadn't stayed in touch with her childhood friends after she'd moved in with Aunt Eileen, either. It would seem Rachel had a history of cutting people off. She doubted she would keep in touch with any of her coworkers from the last firm she had worked at either. But they had never really been close.

Rachel blew some hair out of her eyes and proceeded to the produce department. She was here to start her life fresh. It didn't matter if she was thirty-three and all alone in the entire world. She had been blessed with a good mind. Even if she had lost it for a time. Surely, she could figure things out during this six-month breather she was gifting to herself. Or rather that Aunt Eileen had gifted her.

After all the dust had settled from Todd's debts and life insurance and the sale of their house and the little bit Aunt Eileen had left her, Rachel was fully confident she had enough money to last her at least eight months. That would allow her to live out the required six months here and then, even if she decided she didn't want to stick it out after that, she would have at least two months' worth of funds to start over somewhere new. Since her old employer had promised her she would always have a job there, she would be just fine.

Rachel needed to know she had contingency plans in place. Her dream of becoming a published author was unreliable, she was aware. She would pursue it with all her heart during this six-month sabbatical, but she knew the odds of her succeeding in being able to support herself with her writing were not in her favor. She hadn't been able to find enough solid numbers to actually calculate the odds as she would have liked to, there were just too many variables. But her research had assured her that she needed to have backup plans well in place. Preferably multiple backup plans. Backup plans for her backup plans. And she did. If she decided she wished to stay on the island after all but couldn't make a go of the writing, she could always be a freelance accountant. That thought filled her with the most joy. Being free to do as she wished, wherever she wished, was part of why she wanted to become a full-time author. Well, that and the fact that there were so many stories bouncing around in her head.

But those stories were part of how Todd had convinced her that she was crazy. He said normal people didn't have friends in their head.

"They aren't my friends, Todd," she had tried to explain. "They're just characters. I know they aren't real."

"Doesn't matter, honey," he had said in his overly soothing voice that had used to bring her comfort but later made her stomach clench. "Normal people still don't have people in their head."

She had wanted to argue back that he had no way of knowing that since he wasn't a psychologist, but she had decided it wasn't worth it.

Just remembering those conversations brought a burning sensation to Rachel's midsection and she added antacids to the growing pile in her grocery cart.

A wry smile twisted her lips as she surveyed her cart. She had certainly been seeking comfort as she had shopped, she thought as she pondered the various packages. On further thought, she probably didn't need five bags of potato chips. If she truly needed salty snacks, she would be better off with popcorn, she decided as she returned to that aisle to return at least three of the bags, deciding she would allow herself this first week on the island to wallow in her personal despair.

Chapter Five

What would Daisy be wearing to this ball? Rachel tapped her chin as she stared at the images that turned up from her internet search. The short answer was that it depended. *Well, since I'm Queen of this little world*, Rachel decreed, *I get to say what's what.*

Ball gown 1810 was one of Rachel's favorite search terms. It never failed to turn up the dreamiest concoctions she could describe. Even though she had been attempting to write an historical novel for the last decade and she could probably describe every possible gown any heroine would need, she still loved to do the search and see the images whenever she needed to write a description. It was part of the fun and one of the things she loved the most about her new, temporary, but hopefully permanent one day, job.

Unfortunately, it wasn't the only temporary job she had undertaken. Whether she wanted to live in Sandpiper Cottage or decided to sell it, the poor old house needed some upkeep. Apparently her new, second-favorite website was the one with all the videos for various home repairs. And this afternoon's project was turning out to be a bigger job than she had thought it would be. Perhaps she needed a handyman. It would eat into her budget, but she had been generous in her calculations to allow for some treats. If she ate out less, she should be able to hire someone to do a few of the bigger tasks, especially any that might involve electricity or plumbing. And for sure she needed to hire an expert for the reconstruction of the pier. She had a healthy respect for the water and knew she wouldn't have the nerves to take on at least the foundational work of that particular project.

How was she going to find a handyman on Cape Avalon? She supposed the same way as she found out anything else, search the internet.

Jake Callaghan?

There was no way possible he could be back on the island and the only handyman with a website! Rachel wondered what she could have ever done to deserve what life had been throwing at her that year. She had thought it had been the worst so far, but apparently things could get even worse. Maybe she could hire someone from off-island. But if she had to pay their ferry fees, it would eat so much more into her budget.

Perhaps she could ask around and get some referrals. Surely there were other handymen. They just might not have websites. In a small community, it was possible advertising was unnecessary even in this modern age, she assured herself with a suppressed shudder. Or she could just keep doing these tasks herself.

When a clump of plaster dropped from the ceiling and hit her in the head, though, Rachel put down her tools and left the room. She would ask her neighbors for a recommendation. She had to return Evelyn's casserole dish anyway; she could kill two birds with one stone. What a dreadful expression, Rachel thought with a shudder even as she patted herself off hoping to remove as much dust as possible.

"What a delightful surprise." Rachel was surprised by the other woman's exuberant reaction to finding her on the other side of her door. Again, the woman sounded more southern than she would have expected. "I was hoping you would stop by but was trying not to hold my breath."

Rachel held up the casserole dish as an excuse. "Thank you so much for the delicious and generous welcome. It sure came in handy as it took me a couple days to get to the store and everything filed away."

"I figured, and after the long drive, too. It's always best to have a home cooked, creamy, hot something, isn't it?"

"I haven't had a great deal of experience with that, but I sure did appreciate the gesture. Thank you again."

Finally, Evelyn took the dish from her hand. She had seemed reluctant to do so and Rachel wondered if she had hoped to keep Rachel there as long as possible.

"I don't suppose I could persuade you to stay for a cup of coffee. You probably have a better brand than I do."

Rachel's eyebrows inched toward her hairline. She had thought *she* had shattered confidence, but this poor woman sounded even more insecure than Rachel felt.

"I'm not too much of a coffee snob to accept a cup whenever it's offered. If it isn't too much trouble. There was actually something I was hoping to talk to you about."

It felt to Rachel as though she had just told the other woman she had won the lottery.

"I'll have it ready in a jiffy," she declared with a girlish giggle that belied the few strands of grey and the lines that were bracketing her eyes. "Please, make yourself comfortable and tell me how I can be of help."

Rachel finally took a moment to glance around and wasn't surprised to see the house was immaculate and chicly decorated. She ought to take notes to get some ideas for her own place. She had never really been one for décor and fuss. But she needed to do something with the place. And she wanted to. She was determined to turn over every new leaf there possibly could be turned.

"Excuse the mess," Evelyn called from the kitchen into which she had disappeared. Rachel rolled her eyes, grateful the other woman couldn't see her. What mess? That was all that was missing. Evelyn's head would explode if she could see Sandpiper Cottage.

A quick look around showed Rachel that Evelyn's tidy home had been recently renovated and was quite lovely despite being smaller than her own space. Rachel hadn't thought about how big the cottage was as it was so familiar. But it was the biggest space she had ever lived in. Especially as an adult. That wasn't hard considering she had been living in dorms and apartments for many of the years since she'd been away from the island.

Rachel and Todd had enjoyed being students, so they had both done post graduate studies. That had necessitated keeping expenses as low as possible. Rachel had always thought they had done an excellent job of that and hadn't worried about their future. Material things weren't such a priority for her. She would rather have experiences. She had truly believed Todd had agreed. It was just one of the many things she had been mistaken about her husband.

Evelyn's return to the room coincided with Rachel's sigh. Heat flooded her, but she didn't bother excusing herself. She had never been one to over share. Or even under share. And she wasn't going to unburden herself to this new acquaintance.

30

"I'm sorry to keep you waiting so long," Evelyn began excusing, setting Rachel's teeth slightly on edge. What did this woman have to be so insecure about? Even Rachel wasn't that bad despite everything she had been through. But then, she reminded herself, after everything she had been through, she knew not to judge someone else. Most couldn't possibly know what Rachel had experienced in life. Appearances really meant nothing. She ought to be holding onto compassion for this sweet, generous woman.

"Not at all." Rachel finally mustered the manners she had been raised with. "I've been enjoying your lovely home and views. And taking a few notes for some updates I'd like to do at my place."

Once again, Rachel felt as though she had unknowingly granted this woman a wish.

"Are you planning to make some changes? Eileen would have been so pleased. She knew she ought to do some things, but she felt she couldn't be bothered. And then she got sick and couldn't do it anyway. What are you thinking of doing? And can I help? Oh, do say I can help! It's the thing I would love most." Evelyn appeared to be nearly dancing with the thought. Rachel had to laugh.

"That is a very generous offer. You have no idea what you're getting yourself into."

"Oh, I do, I really do. We completely redid this place, and it was the most fun I've had in years." There was a brief moment of silence while Evelyn seemed to try to gulp back some of her enthusiasm. "Of course, at the time, I had hoped this would be our dream home into which we would welcome our dream children, but at least the renovations were fun."

"I'm sorry," Rachel said, even though she wasn't completely sure what she was apologizing for. It was evident though that she had been right to correct herself from her judgment of the other woman. Obviously, there were pains in her past that Rachel couldn't know. But she could guess. She hesitated to guess at Evelyn's age, but surely it wasn't yet too late for them to have children if that was what she was hoping for. Of course, if they had been trying and it hadn't happened, the odds of it working out would not improve as more time passed. Rachel bit back her smile. Always thinking of maths. It wouldn't do to smile when the other woman was nearly breaking down in front of her.

"Well, in that case, if you aren't too busy, I would welcome some assistance from time to time, or at least some advice. That was actually one of the things I wanted to ask you about. Do you know any good handymen?"

"Jake Callaghan is the best," Evelyn answered promptly, unaware of the inner strife she was causing her guest. "And one could argue the only handyman. Many come from off island, but he's the only full-time resident who does such things. And he's really good at everything I've seen him put his hand to, so you won't go wrong with him if he can fit you into his schedule."

Rachel hoped she was hiding her feelings well. She didn't want to have to explain to Evelyn why she suddenly felt like throwing up all over her lovely cream-colored rugs. She couldn't hire Jake. It would be the absolute epitome of all the reasons why she had sworn never to return. Even the thought of having him working on her house made her feel lightheaded for the briefest moment.

And then she blinked herself back to sense. She was a grown woman. Anything that had happened to her on this island was more than a decade ago. And really, when one considered the entire high school experience from the lens of grown adult perspective, it wasn't such a dreadful experience.

Even though deep in her heart, Rachel blamed Jake for the choices she later made and the dreadful results that created in her life, objectively speaking, Jake was not to blame for the way Todd treated her. The two men had never even met. In fact, Todd knew very little about Rachel's life on Cape Avalon. She needed to pull herself together.

That didn't mean she needed to hire Jake Callaghan. But it did mean she wasn't going to throw up on Evelyn's rug. She cleared her throat and hopefully her facial expression.

"Is there a second best in case Callaghan is too busy for me?"

Evelyn wrinkled her nose. "I wouldn't suggest going with second best, Rachel. But I'll ask around if you'd like."

"I would really appreciate it."

Evelyn looked thrilled with the assigned task. Her eyes were practically glowing as she passed Rachel a steaming cup of coffee and then sat down to sip at her own.

"Tell me everything," she demanded before she suddenly became self-conscious. "About your renovation ideas, of course. I don't mean to pry. You don't have to tell me, if you don't want to."

Rachel forced a light laugh even as her heart went out to the other woman. She herself was feeling desperate for friends, but it would seem her neighbor was in much the same boat. Sympathy welled in her and she was determined to make an effort to be friendly even if she didn't really know how to be a friend.

"It's far from a state secret. For the most part, I only intend a slight facelift. I think the house has held up very well for being on the shores like it is. There is evidence of a few leaks here and there over the years."

"Oh yes, Eileen had the shingles replaced a year and a half ago."

"That will save me so much hassle," Rachel agreed. "But it looks like there's some damage to the ceiling in a couple of places that was never looked after. So, I'll want to check in the attic to make sure there's no decay in there. Or mold. I would hate for there to be mold. Also, there are a few drippy faucets. I've been watching videos to figure out how to fix those myself." She sighed a little. "And the pier is the big thing. I don't feel confident in my ability to repair that in a way that will last in ocean surf. Everything else I feel pretty good about my own abilities. But not that project."

Evelyn was nodding enthusiastically along with everything Rachel was saying. "What about the kitchen and bathrooms? Will you do any upgrades or just a scrub and some paint?"

"Again, I'm happy with the bones of the place. Thankfully Eileen made rather timeless choices when she picked things like tile and flooring. And the cabinetry is of excellent quality. I'm going to research how to refinish the cupboard doors in the kitchen."

"How will you have time for all these projects? Don't you have to work?"

"I've taken a sabbatical. I have six months to figure out what I want to do with my life."

Evelyn nodded again, her facial expression a mixture of sympathy and delight. "It's a good time for a fresh start," she agreed with enthusiasm. "Don't ever hesitate to call on me whenever you want some help. I'm not working right now either and the time hangs heavy on my hands periodically."

Rachel smiled and nodded, taking a last gulp of her coffee and getting to her feet. "I should get out of your hair now, especially since you weren't expecting me."

"No need to rush. Please, come over any time."

Rachel smiled again but didn't allow the other woman's neediness to hold her there. She had her own issues and couldn't get bogged down in whatever was going on with Evelyn. Maybe when she felt on more stable ground herself, she assured herself as she made good her escape with a promise to return another day.

Chapter Six

E velyn watched out her window as Rachel made her way along the path to her aunt's house. Or rather her own house, Evie supposed. She admired the younger woman's slim form but also thought she might perhaps be a bit too thin. Another casserole might be in order. With a shake of her head, Evelyn dismissed the thought. She didn't think Rachel really welcomed interference, and her husband wouldn't appreciate her expending herself in such a way.

She was supposed to be resting. That was why she wasn't working. They had the money for one more try. But Evie had to be fully ready physically before they went ahead with it.

The only problem was, Evelyn didn't think it was a physical problem anymore. Or maybe it was. But being anxious and bored certainly wasn't going to help her get pregnant even with all the miraculous interventions of modern medicine.

The fact that she wanted to feed the neighborhood was just one more piece of evidence that she was meant to be a mother. If only a baby would stay in her womb long enough to live outside of it.

Evelyn bustled back to the kitchen. Perhaps a batch of cookies would be just the thing. She shouldn't eat them herself, though, she cautioned as she pulled the mixer down from the cupboard. Her doctor had already told her she needed to maintain a happy medium with her weight. Not too thin, but Evie needed to make sure she didn't pack on the pounds, either. Her womb was a risky enough host; she needed to keep it as healthy as possible.

But surely a few cookies wouldn't hurt anyone. Evelyn was sure the neighborhood children would be happy if they were to find out she had baked. She could always just go for more or longer walks to make up for it. The doctor had said she needed to exercise.

Not too much though.

Even as she fell into the rhythm of baking Evelyn sighed. There were so many rules. Why did some women pop out babies with alarming frequency and with seemingly no limitations while she couldn't manage to bring one child into the world? She didn't think she was asking too much of the universe. Just one baby, that was all. Why did it have to be so difficult?

The scent of vanilla helped clear her mind and she was soon restored to her equilibrium.

She would have to call Jake and tell him about Rachel's projects. Evelyn was sure he would want to squeeze her new neighbor into his schedule even if he was too busy. Tapping her chin, Evelyn wondered if she was turning into a busybody. With a shrug, she dismissed the thought. What did it matter? Enough people felt sorry for her, they would put up with her managing ways. She vowed to get over it as soon as there was a baby in her arms.

Chapter Seven

Rachel's hand hovered over the door knob. It was the one room she hadn't yet been able to enter and assess. But it felt like she was violating her aunt's privacy. It also felt like if she went in there it would be final. Rachel wasn't yet ready to accept that Aunt Eileen was never coming home. If she didn't go in that room, she could continue to pretend that any minute her aunt would come home, and it would all be better.

Turning away from the door, Rachel continued on to the back of the house. She had plaster to repair. Other things could continue to wait.

Dust swirled in the air, coating everything. With a huff of breath Rachel looked at the open doorway and groaned. She would have to clean the entire house. Again. Then she shrugged. It wasn't as though she had all that much else to do. Even her novel wasn't cooperating at the moment. With another groan, she put her elbows back into her task. If she finished sanding this wall she could maybe paint by the end of the week. If she could finally pick a color.

It wasn't just her aunt's room that was causing her difficulties. Rachel was having trouble with making any changes in the house. A part of her wanted to change everything as a way of starting fresh. The other part wanted to keep it all exactly the way it had always been.

But then Rachel kept reminding herself that her aunt had always talked about making changes in the house, and Sandpiper Cottage was now her own even if she wasn't yet ready to accept the loss of her aunt. And so, she kept right on sanding the rough edges of the plaster she had inexpertly applied the day before.

Despite her conflicted feelings on the subject of the renovations, it was the first time in years that she had the sensation of pride in herself. She was managing to get projects finished. The faucets no longer dripped. The window in the second bedroom opened smoothly without squeaking. There wasn't a single cobweb in the entire house. Except maybe Aunt Eileen's room. Rachel couldn't be sure of the state of that particular room.

In between projects and YouTube viewing, Rachel made an effort to get in her words each day. She was determined to stick with a writing schedule, even if it was only a minimum of 500 words. Usually, she could do that much while her morning coffee brewed which was also adding to her sense of accomplishment. She was filled with joy over the direction her story was going, even if it wasn't as speedy as she would prefer.

There was no one to squelch that sensation. Except her own sense of self-worth or lack thereof. But she was doing her best to ignore that voice. She had read the expression to write drunk and edit sober. While she didn't actually drink in the mornings before doing her writing, she tried to maintain the writers high of accomplishment. It filed her with a deep sense of joy that she couldn't remember ever feeling before.

Perhaps when she was a child and didn't know the tragedies that awaited her, she mused as she walked on the beach one afternoon while the primer dried.

She had begun to keep track of the tides. Of course, they had always been there; she was certain high and low tides were not new phenomena. She just hadn't bothered to pay them any attention when she last lived here. A shake of her head accompanied that thought. She had been a dolt as a youth. About so many things, she acknowledged with a sigh. And poor Aunt Eileen had put up with her through it all.

In any case, Rachel was determined to focus on the positive going forward with her life. So, she was thrilled to now be aware and watchful of the tides. It amazed her that they changed time every day. She also hoped that one day she would know it off by heart but for now, she faithfully checked the tidal website to confirm when the lowest tides would be. It tickled her to walk along the beach when the water was at its lowest point. Even in the blustery weather of near winter. The stretch of sand felt so expansive. And then too there were often intriguing things to take note of in the little pools that formed as the water receded. Things you wouldn't normally be able to see, that ought to be at the bottom of the ocean but were left on the beach when the water went away temporarily.

She was strangely fascinated by the barnacles. She thought their tenacity was admirable. She only wished she could develop a degree of their ability to stick with it.

She needed to be a barnacle. The thought made her smile. At least for the next five months she was planted here at Aunt Eileen's house. And she was determined to stick with her decision to get a book published.

It was well known that everyone wished to write a book. Rachel herself had volumes of notebooks with half-written story ideas. She even had a few manuscripts on her computer in various stages of development. But she had never actually finished one.

She placed a lot of the blame on Todd and his strange habit of undermining her confidence. But perhaps he had been right. She had never actually completed a single manuscript. A part of her suspected it was an emotional crutch. She had come to care deeply about every single character she had ever created. Rachel wondered if perhaps she feared that completing their stories would end that relationship somehow. And perhaps it would in a certain way. But just as she hoped for a happy ending for herself, she really ought to provide some endings for some of these beloved characters.

A grin split her face. She hadn't even completed a single manuscript and here she was turning into a crazy creative, thinking her characters were real people with feelings and futures. Maybe Todd had been right after all. But she now knew enough authors, at least digitally, to know she wasn't the only crazy person with characters in her head.

Staring out over the vast ocean before her, Rachel nodded to herself. Perhaps they were real, at least in the environs of her own imagination. And the thought of the sense of accomplishment that she would feel if she ever did manage to get any of them publishable filled her with a sense of purpose. A surge of energy at the very thought flooded her and she hopped to her feet, no longer as interested in the barnacles. She was going to be one herself. Those crusty creatures could look after themselves.

Her purposeful strides ate up the distance between the cove and the cottage. She would start working on the submission requirements for the agents she had researched. Surely that would be the kick in the backside she required to actually finish one of her projects. And the agents didn't need to know the manuscript wasn't yet fully completed. As long as the first pages that they allowed you to submit were polished up, that gave her time to finish the rest. From everything she had read in all the forums, it could take ages and ages to hear back, if you ever did. She didn't want to waste time now that she was fired up.

Besides, she had to decide what she was doing with her life by the end of her six-month commitment to stay on Cape Avalon. If she was going to have to get a job, she wanted to be confident that she had done everything in her power to achieve her dreams first.

A new story idea was starting to form in her head. That always filled her with the tingles. But she was determined to complete the stories she had already begun first. She pulled out her cell phone and opened a note taking app. She would get to the new idea one day soon.

Her fingers were itching to start flying on the keyboard but first, she checked on her paint. Still a bit too damp for a second coat. She had time to write. What a shame about the paint, the sarcastic thought twisting her lips into a smirk, and then time slipped away as she immersed herself in the current story.

Minutes or hours later Rachel was tapping her chin with one finger as she stared at her screen. What should the smugglers be bringing into the country? Liquor would be expected, but who wants to be predictable? Wool was also a commodity the smugglers brought in illegally to avoid taxes. That might be a fascinating twist to the story.

A glance at the clock, though, told Rachel she had already gone down enough rabbit holes of research that day and she needed to get back to her other important project. She jotted down a couple notes of where she thought the story was going and closed down her laptop. It would be easy for her to pick up again when she was ready.

Both projects were important. She was determined to maintain the house. Rachel knew how much Aunt

Eileen had always loved it. It had been a surprise to see the state it had gotten into, despite what she had told Evelyn. It was obvious Aunt Eileen had been far sicker than she had ever let on to Rachel. Or at least sick for much longer than she had admitted to.

Guilt ate away at Rachel's belly. She ought to have visited despite her youthful vow and her husband's interference. Maturity should have allowed her to see that such a vow had been rash and probably baseless. She was here now, and the sky hadn't fallen. She hadn't even yet run into anyone from school, other than Tina. Of course, she had only been there for three weeks and the only places she had gone were the grocery and hardware stores, but still, if disaster had been on the verge of striking her surely, she would have known about it.

But there was also the fact that she had wanted to keep her troubles with Todd away from Aunt Eileen. So, they had developed a routine of sorts of meeting each other in destination cities. It had been wonderful to travel with her beloved relative. She had such happy memories of their last trip in New York nine months ago. Rachel couldn't believe Eileen had been so able to hide her illness from her even then. But the fact that Rachel never came home had also allowed Eileen to hide her challenges just as Rachel had been hiding her own. A deep sigh erupted from Rachel, seemingly travelling all the way from her toes.

She ought to have done better.

And that was the crux of her pain right now. What if Aunt Eileen never knew how much Rachel loved her? Rachel almost doubled over with the pain of that thought. Aunt Eileen was dead. All she had left of her aunt was this house. It didn't take a Freudian diagnosis to recognize that Rachel's determination to fix up and beautify the aging home was out of a desire to please her last beloved, but sadly deceased, relative.

On the other hand, though, it didn't hurt to have a lovely beach home for free. Rachel reminded herself of her resolve to look on the brighter side of things. It had been one final act of love on Eileen's part to leave her the house, even though she knew Rachel didn't want to be on the island. She had known Rachel needed the island. Or at least somewhere safe to hole up for a bit while she figured out her life.

That too was an issue Rachel needed to deal with eventually. The state of her marriage. Or rather the state it had been in when her husband had died suddenly. No one's death should be considered a relief, so Rachel tried not to think that. But she wasn't sorry Todd was gone from her life. It had been a toxic situation for her. Perhaps from the very beginning of the relationship, but certainly in recent years. Rachel didn't yet have enough mental clarity or distance to decide when the problems had truly crept in.

She was probably going to need to consult with a professional to truly get past all her baggage. But for now, she would stay in hibernation at the cottage for a little while longer.

Rachel actually liked the imagery evoked by thinking of her stay there as hibernation. Perhaps she ought to think of it as a metamorphosis. She was mixing metaphors here, but she was determined to emerge as a butterfly when the hibernation period was over.

Even if she had to return to accounting, Rachel would make sure that she had altered everything else in her life, most of all her perspective. And if she could make her peace with the island, she would find remote work to keep the lights on. She felt the closest to her family here in this house, even though they were all gone now. She supposed it was because the bulk of her memories were centered around this lovely house.

Her parents had loved visiting her father's sister at Sandpiper Cottage and had brought Rachel at least once or twice each year before their untimely death when she was thirteen years old. So, it hadn't been such a shock to her system when she had come to live with Aunt Eileen, even though she had acted as though it was. Rachel worked at forgiving her younger self. Losing your parents at that age would throw anyone for a loop. Perhaps Eileen should have made sure she got some counselling. But there was no changing the past at this point. Eileen had done her best even though Rachel hadn't.

Rachel put aside the project she was working on for the time being. She was happy with what she had accomplished thus far in the room. Even though she had only learned from videos online, she was pretty happy with the way the plastering had turned out. Even if you looked close, you could no longer see the cracks that had been marring the wall before. But now her thoughts were too distressful and circling too frantically around her mind. She needed a steady hand for painting the trim where it met the wall, and she couldn't do that while she was fretting over the disaster she had allowed to become of her life.

While she was doing her best to focus on the positive and look to the future, it might be time for her to process some of her past as well. But she couldn't do that and paint, too. The beach was calling to her even if it was a blustery cold day.

After wrapping a scarf firmly around her neck and tugging a hat down over her ears, Rachel made her way down to the beach. It wasn't low tide yet, but she didn't need the beach to delight her that day, she just needed to walk off her nerves.

Her restless thoughts chased her much further than she usually walked, and she was surprised to look up and realize she had walked all the way to the point. The lighthouse was faithfully flashing its light even though it wasn't near to falling dark. She had made fast time, and the tide was now fully out. The sharp and dangerous rocks that made up the point and the purpose of the lighthouse to protect unsuspecting boaters were on full display. If it wasn't so cold out Rachel would love to wade out to them and explore. It wasn't often you could see them so clearly as today. But it was much too cold for that. Perhaps in the spring or early summer, before her six-month stay was up, she would time it right and get to see for herself. For now, the tumble and splash of the waves slapping themselves against the sturdy rocks was a satisfying background to her thoughts. Rachel found a protected cove to sit in and allowed her mind free rein.

Todd hadn't been the most handsome young man she'd met during her freshman year, but he was close. Tall and slim with an earnest look about him, Rachel had felt both safe and energized in his company. It had turned out that impression was an illusion, but it had lasted for years. They had shared many of the same classes and interests.

Being only seventeen due to skipping a grade, Rachel was at least a year younger in age and perhaps even more so in life experience than most of her classmates. Todd had seemed like a safe confidante to her young eyes.

They had become almost inseparable by the end of her first year. It had been a solid friendship that then turned romantic. Even with the clarity of hindsight, Rachel was certain there had been a purity to their early relationship. She hadn't really known how to develop relationships; Todd had become her entire world. It had happened gradually but by the time they graduated from university, it had seemed so natural that they would marry.

She had studied business and accounting rather than psychology, so she couldn't explain what had led to the change in Todd, but at some point he stopped being a supportive partner and became increasingly domineering and demeaning. Rachel was certain he hadn't started demoralizing her until after they'd been married a few years. Perhaps it was because he was so disappointed in himself that he had felt the need to undercut her accomplishments. For several years they had worked for the same firm. When Rachel had received a promotion that he had hoped for, that became a festering wound between them.

When she had been head-hunted to another firm, Rachel had hoped that it would be better for them, there would be less direct competition between them, but just the fact that another company had wanted her rather than him had probably rankled in Todd's evidently immature psyche.

Her interest in writing Historical Romance novels had just been an added point of derision for Todd. Maybe if she had ever managed to finish a manuscript, he would have seen that it wasn't such a ridiculous idea. But his snide comments had made it challenging for her to ever accomplish what she had set out to do.

Not this time, though. This time, Rachel was determined to only have supportive voices in her head. It was hard enough to fight her own insecurities. It was a relief not to have anyone else adding to them.

Guilt swept through her and she kicked at the sand under feet. She shouldn't be relieved that her husband was dead. She ought to be sorry. And she was, of course. They had been the best of friends at one point. He had helped her deal with being away from the island and had helped her adjust to college life. They had been so in tune at one point in their history.

Even if none of that were true, though, he had been a person who didn't deserve to die so young. The fact that he had left her nearly destitute didn't change the fact that he had been a human life. And if she hadn't let her insecurities and issues get in the way, she would have stayed on top of their finances and known what he was doing. He hadn't really tried very hard to hide it. It had all come out easily at his death. If she hadn't stopped checking their bank statements, she might have known and could have perhaps even gotten him help. Obviously, he must have become addicted to gambling to have run up so much debt in those online games.

If she hadn't retreated into her own shell, she might have realized he had turned into a different person. Or rather, she had noticed and retreated from that person. That wasn't what a friend, a wife, ought to do with the person she had vowed to love until death did they part.

Well, now, death had parted them, and she would have to learn to forgive them both for the mistakes they'd each made in the past. And she would do better in the future.

Not that she would ever remarry. And she couldn't get her parents or her aunt back either. But once she was done licking her wounds metaphorically, Rachel was determined to turn her face outward and try to make friends. And be a friend to those new friends. Perhaps she ought to start with her neighbor. Evelyn had been so eager to help her and delighted at Rachel's request for information.

While she hadn't yet started to engage any of her neighbors in conversations and still dreaded that eventual occurrence, she made small strides and had become "waving acquaintances" with many who enjoyed her stretch of beach. She had even begun to recognize who lived where and which dog belonged with which people. She hadn't felt like actually conversing with anyone, but it was sort of nice to feel a little bit of camaraderie with the neighborhood.

It was time for Rachel to stop isolating herself and start reaching out to others.

Okay, maybe almost time. She had a right to her own grieving process, she assured herself.

But she would keep it in mind and try. Soon.

Rachel had forgotten her phone back at the house so wasn't completely sure how much time had passed since she'd sat there, but the level of the water relative to those formerly huge boulders led her to believe she had sat there longer than she had planned. The inclement weather must have kept everyone else home today. Not a single other person had disturbed her mental wanderings.

Getting to her feet and brushing the sand off her backside, Rachel admired anew the ever-changing seascape. The sound of the waves, the freshness in the air, the sunshine overhead; it all combined to do something deep inside her. Healing what she hadn't even known was broken. Despite her dour thoughts while she'd sat there, Rachel smiled as she admired the view a little longer before turning her back on it and setting out toward her house.

At least she had made a little progress. She was thinking of Sandpiper Cottage as her own now rather than continually referring to it in her mind as Aunt Eileen's house. It probably helped that her aunt had made her feel so at home when she'd moved there at the age of thirteen. So, it had felt like home for years before she turned her back on it in such a rash way at the age of seventeen.

Rachel shook off the unhelpful thoughts with a sigh. She was back to castigating herself. It was ridiculous. Every seventeen-year-old did rash things, she was sure. Not that she knew any now, but her schoolmates had all been doing ridiculous things. That was part of why she had made her own rash declaration.

While she was working on doling out forgiveness to herself and Todd, she ought to consider doing so for her former classmates as well.

She didn't know if she could dig deep enough into her heart to find forgiveness for Jake Callaghan, though. That might be asking too much.

Chapter Eight

J ake. Just the name brought certain images to her mind. Images of a good-looking young man in well-worn blue jeans and well fitted t-shirts. As a thirty-three-year-old woman it felt a little lecherous to think of the teenager she'd once known in such terms, but she gave herself a mental shrug. She had been a teenager then, too.

Jake Callaghan was two years older than her. She supposed he still was, she thought with a small smile. That would make him thirty-five. She wondered how he'd aged. Did he have a dad bod and thinning hair or had he continued to maintain the lean physique he'd had as a boy? She supposed working construction would help keep him fit. Unless he'd enjoyed too much beer as had been a common tendency amongst their peers when they were in high school.

Because Rachel had skipped the fifth grade before her parents had died, and Jake had failed a grade somewhere along his school boy journey, they were in the same class when Rachel moved in with Aunt Eileen.

Rachel suspected that she had appeared as some sort of challenge to the other teenagers when she had turned up at their school all solemn and sullen in her grief. She and Jake had struck up a mutually respectful hatred of one another.

With the hindsight of maturity, as well as some sessions with a therapist, Rachel was pretty sure they were probably both feeling insecure about their age in the class. Rachel was uncomfortable with the brainiac label she was immediately pinned with, and it probably felt awkward for the fifteen-year-old young man to be in a classroom full of kids younger than him, especially the thirteen-year-old girl who still looked like a child.

But Rachel had grown comfortable with her brainy status and had thrown herself into her schooling. She didn't skip any more grades, as all the teachers agreed she needed to cover all the subjects, but each of the teachers in their community school had made an effort to keep her stimulated intellectually, finding advance placement courses for her even if she was the only student in them.

It was inevitable that she would be the valedictorian of their graduating class. What wasn't inevitable was the way some of her classmates had treated her in that final year. At the time it had been devastating to her. In the grand scheme of life's challenges, it really wasn't that big of a deal, but when Jake and his friends had mocked her while she was giving her final speech at their graduation ceremony, it had felt like her world was crumbling around her, and so she had left that auditorium and gone home to pack her bags, leaving the next morning, early for college, vowing to never set foot back on the island.

Eileen had tried to be supportive but hadn't been able to talk her out of leaving, so she had unhappily driven her to school, finding Rachel somewhere to stay for the few weeks she was there before the summer session she had already planned to attend started.

It was rash in that it punished both her and her aunt and probably didn't affect her stupid classmates in the least. Rachel would bet she had never even crossed their minds in the decade and a half that had passed since that dreadful night.

But even with the realization that it had been rash, Rachel still wasn't sorry that she hadn't seen Jake in all that time and didn't look forward to the possibility of running into him in the least. In fact, despite Evelyn's recommendation of hiring Jake to help with her renovations, Rachel had yet to make the call. She was of the opinion that she would rather let the old pier disappear completely into the Atlantic than to have that man to her home. Guilt continued to niggle at her, though. Aunt Eileen never complained about her health or her circumstances, but she had frequently mentioned that she wished she could get around to fixing the pier. At the time, whenever Eileen had mentioned it during visits or phone calls, Rachel had thought she was too busy to deal with it. It hadn't occurred to her that her beloved aunt was too sick to take on the project.

The fact that she had mentioned it more than once, though was telling. And Rachel felt she owed it to her dearest relative to have the repairs done in her honor. If only that didn't entail hiring Jake.

Perhaps she would be able to find the second best option, as Evelyn had mentioned.

But Sandpiper Cottage deserved better than second best.

A sigh escaped her as she neared her own backyard. Or perhaps front yard. Rachel wasn't completely certain how to refer to the beachside area of her house. In a city, the area with the driveway, the road side would be considered the front yard. But in this case, with the ocean just steps away, Rachel would be willing to consider that the front. English was such a funny language.

"Hello there."

She nearly jumped out of her skin she was so startled by the sudden sound of a voice off to her right. Rachel had once again allowed herself to become so wrapped up in her own thoughts that she had lost connection with her surroundings. She ought to not let that keep happening.

Squinting into the sunlight, Rachel couldn't see who had called out to her. In fact, she was assuming he had called out to her, but she didn't recognize the deep, warm voice as any of her neighbors. Not that she had actually spoken with any of the neighbors she thought, as another wave of guilt chipped away at her self-confidence.

A quick glance around told Rachel that she was the only other person in her vicinity, although she couldn't be sure he wasn't with someone else. But if he was, it was unlikely he would be calling out in such a way. Taking a deep breath, Rachel hoped her face looked pleasant despite her inner turmoil as she waved in lieu of a response to his greeting.

"Rachel?"

Nerves tingled down her limbs as the deep voice called out her name. How did he know her? Did she know him? Then dread clawed at the back of her neck. It couldn't be Jake. Had she conjured him with her earlier thoughts? Or was her mind playing tricks on her?

She lifted her hand to her eyebrow hoping to shield her eyes so she could see better, but since he was up on the dune with the sun almost directly behind him, she couldn't see clearly. The craven part of her wanted to put her head down and keep walking, as though she hadn't heard him at all.

But she had already waved.

"Tough times don't last; tough people do." *She whispered to herself.* "I am capable. I am strong. I believe in myself." *Big breath in.*

The silly chants brought a smile to her lips and calmed some of her inner turmoil. Pulling back her shoulders and lifting her chin, Rachel took a deep breath and reminded herself that she was a grown-up now. One that had graduated from university with multiple degrees and been successful in her field. No one needed to know that certain aspects of her life had been less than successful. And she was on a hiatus from beating herself up. She also wouldn't allow anyone else to do it for her.

"Can I help you?" she finally called out, still unable to identify the speaker and not comfortable getting close enough to do so.

He must have realized she didn't recognize him as the man quickly made short work of descending the dune into her path. She wasn't used to being around such well-formed men. He seemed large and imposing. Rachel wanted to step back but stood her ground firmly.

When he was no longer in stark relief with the sun, Rachel grew even more convinced that her first impression had been correct. Jake Callaghan hadn't changed very much in the last fifteen years. Except that he had filled out even more. Her impression of a well-built, wide-shouldered man had been accurate. Clearly, working in construction had prevented any midlife spread so far. And her wish of him losing his thick, luscious hair hadn't been granted either. She almost reached up self-consciously toward her own messy ponytail but caught the tell-tale sign of nerves before she could give it away.

"Jake," she finally said in lieu of any other greeting.

"I thought that was you. I'd heard you'd returned to the island."

"You have, have you? That's odd, since I haven't talked to anyone." Rachel didn't need the awkward reminder that small town life was a gossipy one. All her warm thoughts about living in her aunt's house started to seep away.

"Tina saw you at the Pick and Pack," Jake said, reminding her of that briefly awkward encounter. "Also, Evelyn has been quite excited about her new neighbor," Jake explained with a grin. "She mentioned you might need some help with some upgrades on your house?"

"And you thought to offer your services?" Rachel asked with little inflection. "Evelyn mentioned you were likely too busy to fit me into your schedule. I was planning to call around to others."

"There aren't many others," Jake replied, not seeming to notice her responses were far cooler than his greetings. "I happened to be in the area and thought I'd stop by and see what you were working on. I haven't seen you since graduation. How have you been?"

Nausea roiled in her belly, and she couldn't answer him. Before the silence grew too awkward though, he suddenly appeared contrite.

"Of course, you haven't been great with losing your aunt. And Evelyn mentioned your husband recently also died," he quickly said, sounding sincerely sorry. "I am so sorry for your losses. Each would have been tough, but both so soon one right after the other must be terrible. I was really sorry to hear about it."

Obviously the island had been abuzz with her news if he knew about both deaths. Even though she hadn't yet talked to anyone directly, it would seem she had been the topic of conversation amongst her neighbors. The thought embarrassed her immensely. But he sounded sincere, and a lump formed in Rachel's throat despite her best efforts to have no reaction at all to him. She hated that he was so fit and handsome and confident while she was a blubbering mess, at least on the inside even if she was managing to keep her grief to herself.

Clearing her throat as delicately as she could manage helped Rachel get her voice back. She couldn't look him fully in the face, so she kept her gaze somewhere around his shoulder.

"I don't think I'll be needing to hire any help for the time being, Jake, but thank you for stopping in to see."

"Are you sure? Do you have any renovation experience? Evelyn said you might need the pier looked at."

Rachel tried not to feel furious with Evelyn. The poor woman was trying to be helpful and had no way of knowing how Rachel would feel about this. Rachel had, in fact, asked about contractors, so Evelyn couldn't even be accused of being a busy body on this topic, even though Rachel had mentioned she would consider other contractors instead. She had allowed Evelyn to think it was because that woman had mentioned Jake's busy schedule. So, Rachel fully understood that this was a favor in Evelyn's mind. Perhaps even in Jake's, she realized with a bit of a thud in her midsection. The man probably had absolutely no idea that he had set her on a self-destructive path so long ago.

"I was thinking I might just let the pier finish its journey to destruction. I doubt I'll be buying a boat, especially not one big enough for this side of the island. So, I don't truly need the pier."

Jake was nodding as though agreeing with her to at least an extent. "I can see that. But what about for the sake of beach erosion? It might be better to have something in place to protect your beach and to give you a means of accessing the beach that protects the dunes."

"Wouldn't creating a walkway through the dunes do far more damage than if I just make a careful path?"

"Not if it's done right."

Rachel could hear his confidence oozing from his voice, and she wished quite spitefully that she could relieve him of some of it. But she had always been far too self-contained. Even in her youthful, prideful rage after the graduation, she hadn't told anyone why she was leaving or yelled at the people who had caused her pain the way she had wished to. Even Aunt Eileen hadn't fully understood why she was leaving. So, she wasn't about to start flinging around insults at this juncture of life. But oh, how she wished she were that type.

"Well, thank you for stopping in, Jake, I will think about what you've said and contact you if I have need of your services."

"I could provide you a quote right now, so you'll know what you're looking at." She could hear a little bit of puzzlement in his tone, but she still couldn't look him in the face. He was being reasonable, and she wasn't. She hated that.

"That would probably be a good idea," she finally managed to choke out before breaking the pose of conversation and heading toward the house. Gesturing toward what was left of the old pier she called to him as she walked away. "I need a drink. The pier's over there. You can meet me by the driveway when you're done."

At that point she couldn't even care that she probably ought to offer him some form of hospitality. It wasn't a hot day, so she wasn't humanly required to do so. It was only island hospitality that expected it.

But the man had ruined her life. Surely, she didn't owe him a single thing.

A few minutes later, after washing her face and drinking a large glass of water, Rachel felt much more settled. It was good that she was getting meeting Jake over with. She hadn't left the house much and Rachel realized that part of it was a dread of running into any of the people she had known in school. That was ridiculous. She was planning to be on the island for at least six months. She couldn't stay home for all of them. If she survived this encounter, she was sure she would have greater confidence in her ability to get through any future encounters.

Not that she would consider searching out said encounters. Especially not by hiring Jake Callaghan to repair her pier. The ocean could reclaim her land if it wanted to. Paying Jake to be around would be the height of her own ruin. No one in their right mind could ever expect it of her.

Before she had worked herself up into a total knot on the topic, there was a light tap on the back door, and her stomach squeezed. She had said she'd meet him by the driveway, and she had dithered too long. Throwing back her shoulders Rachel marched to the door, determined to brave through this experience and then get on with her growth process.

It took effort not to be disarmed by the lopsided grin that adorned his face.

"I should have gotten your number from Evelyn so I could make an appointment with you, shouldn't I? You look busy."

Rachel shrugged, trying to look self-assured. "I'm always busy, so now is just as good a time as any," she finally answered somewhat politely. While she didn't really wish to have this meeting, she had been raised to be polite. Only in her head could she tell Jake to scram and not let the door hit him on the way out...

Chapter Nine

I t took all of Jake's considerable strength and courage to climb the stairs and knock on that door. He had seen all the judgment in Rachel's gaze when he had called out to her on the beach. He should have left well enough alone. He should have told Evelyn he was too busy to take on any work for the next millennium when she had told him about Rachel's renovations. Instead, he had hot-footed over to her house like the teenage boy he had been when he'd first met her.

The moment Rachel Whitney walked into his classroom at Avalon Middle School was forever etched on his memory, as though it had happened days ago instead of the two decades that had actually elapsed. She should have been awkward, gangly, and sullen in all her thirteen-year-old glory and grief but instead she had seemed like a lost little elf that he wanted to protect. So instead, being the obnoxious fifteen-year-old that he was, feeling awkward about being a year older and nearly a head taller than everyone else in the class, he'd repudiated those soft and gentle feelings and pulled her braids the first chance he'd gotten.

Of course, he shouldn't have done that to the poor kid, but what had she been thinking to wear her hair in braids at the end of the eighth grade? Yes, she was much younger than everyone else in the class, because, yes, she was far smarter than everyone else in the class. But those smarts should have told her that wearing braids was absolutely the wrong thing to do.

It wasn't until years later that he found out she wore braids in her hair so often because it was a ritual she used to share with her mother who had died in an accident that sent Rachel to live with her aunt on the Cape. The essay Rachel had written for their eleventh grade English class had nearly brought him to tears. Which had only fueled his torment of her.

Jake's chest and face ached with the shame of the difficulty he had caused that young girl. He was well aware that helping the grown-up version of Rachel Whitney renovate her inherited house wasn't going to change what a goon he had been way back then, but it would do a little something to assuage the guilt he had carried around with him since the day of their high school graduation. The expression on Rachel's face was etched into his memory just as indelibly as his first impression of her from their first encounter. He only wished he could replace it with something better. Or erase it completely.

Scratch that. He didn't actually wish to erase his memories of Rachel Whitney. He only wished he could replace them with better ones. Or add better ones now, at the end of the story. Jake shook his head. He was being fanciful again. He supposed that's what came of spending so much time babysitting his niece. She was always going on about fairy tales and happy endings.

Swiping his hand through his hair and then rubbing them both on his jeans when he realized his palms were actually sweaty, Jake tried to dispel his flicker of nerves. He was Jake Callaghan. There was nothing to be nervous about. He had years of experience talking to girls or women. This was just quoting a job. He had done that thousands of times, surely, or at least hundreds. There was nothing to be so nervous about.

Finally, taking his courage in both his metaphorical hands, Jake tapped on the door and nearly groaned at himself. That was not how he normally knocked. He was a purposeful sort. Or he had become one in the last decade or so. He had learned to be a man and get stuff done. Purposefully.

His thoughts brought amusement to his face. Apparently, just being in Rachel Whitney's presence lowered his IQ several points. He couldn't even think in a broad vocabulary. Maybe this was a bad idea. He certainly didn't need the work. And he had managed to go more than fifteen years ignoring his conscience for his youthful failings, surely he could continue to do so with regards to this one woman.

He almost walked away when she didn't answer the door immediately. Evidently, she didn't want to see him any more than he now wanted to see her. But before he could suit thoughts to actions, she was opening the door and staring at him with the same wide gaze she had used on that first day of school.

"You don't wear your hair in braids anymore?"

Jake actually contemplated punching himself in the teeth for that idiotic question. He was pleased and relieved to see that a half smile lifted the corners of her mouth. It wasn't really amusement, but at least it wasn't a frown.

"Not today," was all she said. But at least she didn't take a swing at him. Not that she had ever reacted in a physical way to any of his jokes and teasing in the past. She had merely stared through him in that way she had of making him feel like the dirt beneath her feet. He couldn't quite meet her gaze while he waited for her to say something more.

He felt her soft sigh even though it was barely audible and certainly wasn't gusty enough to have reached him. But he found himself wishing he was the demonstrative type. Jake actually wanted to hug the woman. Perhaps spending time with his niece really had addled his brain. But he could never regret that. That little girl was the best thing in his life. But they had also made him much more aware of female thoughts and feelings. He didn't always understand them, but he was aware of them.

"Did you have something to tell me or are we just enjoying the late afternoon breeze?" Rachel's half smile had finally returned, and she seemed to be tolerating his presence a little better than when he had first surprised her on the dune.

Jake cleared the lump in his throat with a light cough. "The pier has pretty much disappeared, hasn't it?"

"It would seem so. I guess the Atlantic is pretty hard on wooden structures."

Jake nodded. "Most are building retaining walls and piers with reinforced concrete these days. There are special compounds for use in water."

"Sounds complicated and expensive," Rachel countered hesitantly.

"Not any more complicated than a wooden structure," Jake replied. "And not too expensive with the former classmate discount."

With a blink of her pretty hazel gaze her face was devoid of all expression, leaving disappointment tasting bitter on Jake's tongue. "I don't need you to do me any favors, Callaghan," she answered in a cold tone. "I really do think I will just let the pier project wait for another year or two. It's been falling apart for years now, surely there's no amount of urgency."

Jake didn't want to try to force himself on her, but he couldn't let her statement go uncontested.

"With climate change, storms are getting worse in these parts. I'm sure your aunt told you about them." Having mentioned Eileen, now Jake felt awkward. He should have started with mentioning her loss. Or maybe he had. He couldn't remember. He also couldn't remember ever being so nervous to talk to a woman. He cleared his throat again. "I was very sorry to hear about her death, by the way. How are you holding up?"

A mixture of emotions he couldn't even begin to identify flooded across her face before she clamped it down and presented him with another one of her blank expressions. She had learned to do that in high school when he or his friends were teasing her. It seemed as though someone had told her that they were just looking for a reaction so she refused to give it to them. It had creeped him out a little bit as a teenager. Now he admired her self-control. But it also told him that he had struck a nerve.

"I've learned that my life is a never-ending series of losses. But I keep right on ticking," she finally answered him, sounding a little bitter.

Jake no longer wished to prolong the awkward moment despite his still strong desire to offer her the comfort of a hug. He had learned from his nieces that there were never too many hugs from a majority of females' perspective. He doubted Rachel would welcome one from him, but he still believed she needed one. And it seemed like there was no longer anyone in her life to offer them to her.

Despite her prickly surface, his heart went out to her. It was just human compassion, he assured himself, not anything deeper that might be a remnant of his complicated feelings for her as a teen.

"Anyway, about the pier, I'll have to verify the current price of one of the products I'd like to recommend before I really give you the price. Could I get your number or your email address so I could send it to you when I know for sure?"

Reluctance was evident in her posture, but she nodded and reeled off the information quickly. He had to repeat it back to her to make sure he got it right. Again, she hesitated but then nodded and said thank you in her prim, polite voice that brought a grin to Jake's face.

"What all are you doing to the house? Evelyn didn't go into too many details about it. I got the impression she hadn't seen it yet."

Jake's eyebrows arched when Rachel suddenly turned bashful. Pink tinged her previously pale and drawn features, and she actually kicked the deck with the toe of her shoe.

"I haven't had her over yet. I'm the worst neighbor after she's been so sweet to me. I just can't bring myself to do it, somehow."

Jake watched her for a moment before shrugging and nodding at the same time. "That certainly doesn't make you the worst. I have some stories I could tell you about terrible neighbors. But in your case, I would say it has something to do with your losses, doesn't it? You don't want to have company because somewhere in your mind you're just house-sitting your aunt's house, right?"

Surprise showed in her eyes as she finally met his gaze for the first time since she'd opened the door. Jake had to concentrate not to step back from the reaction he felt. There was such an overwhelming force of emotions swirling inside her that she managed to keep from her face for the most part, but her eyes couldn't hide them.

"A little ridiculous, isn't it?" she asked.

"I wouldn't say so. Grief is a tricky thing. Everyone experiences it a bit differently and at different times."

"Evelyn offered to help me and I told her I would welcome the help, but then I avoided her ever since. I really ought to get over it. I'm either going to be staying here or I'll be selling up, but either way, Aunt Eileen is gone and I really ought to be able to accept it. I'm not thirteen anymore, trying to pretend that my parents will come back any minute."

"You've certainly had a tough shake of it, haven't you?" What else could he say? But Jake felt so lack-witted all the same.

To his shock, though, his weak words seemed to amuse her as the first genuine smile stretched her lips and he caught his breath.

"I certainly have. But I have this beautiful house in the most amazing location on the planet, and I'm starting over."

"I bet you never thought you would come home to start over, did you?"

"I did not," she agreed vehemently. "I actually swore I never would."

Jake blinked in surprise. He wasn't actually surprised about her vow, really, since he had never heard of her returning. He was just surprised that she would admit as much to him. Especially since he suspected a large portion of the motivation behind such a vow was him and his childish actions when he should have known better.

"Are you looking for work? Or are you all set in that department? I suppose, a smart girl like you would have ensured her family was well insured."

It was evidently the exact wrong thing to say, as her features tightened before all expression was once more wiped from her face.

"I don't see how that is any of your business, Mr. Callaghan. But thank you for looking into that product for me. I have to get back to things, so I'll wish you a pleasant day."

And with that she stepped back from him, swiftly opened the door, and then shut it in his face, all in a smooth movement as though she had practiced it many times. But he had seen her eyes. And he knew she wasn't emotionless at all. He felt like the worst sort of cad. But all he could do was step away from her porch and leave her be.

Chapter Ten

Rachel collapsed onto the front room sofa in the fetal position. How could an encounter with a man she hadn't seen in over fifteen years chew her up so much? She ought to not care in the least what Jake looked like or thought.

But he looked so handsome and vital, as though energy pulsed within him. And she had seen kindness and compassion in his gaze when she had finally met it briefly. She didn't want Jake Callaghan's compassion. How dare he feel sorry for her? And how dare he ask about her situation? And how dare he be right? Yes, she should have made sure everyone was better insured than they were.

Of course, Todd had been insured. Not spectacularly, but it should have been more than sufficient. If he hadn't racked up an exorbitant amount of debt gambling and somehow managed to take out a second mortgage on their house in order to cover some of it without her knowledge, it would have been plenty. Instead, he left her with nothing after paying off all the debts, or near enough to be the same.

And Aunt Eileen had been in a similar sort of situation. She had been lucky, well, maybe not lucky given the context, but she had purchased her insurance policy long before she had gotten sick, so it didn't exclude her illness. But she had taken out a mortgage on the cottage to pay for some of her treatment expenses. The insurance money had covered all those bills and left a little bit more besides. Rachel was only grateful that Todd hadn't been able to get his hands on any of that. It had only actually been finalized right before he had been killed.

So, Rachel had a very small nest egg, giving her a little safe spot and resting place for at least the six months required to fulfill the residency requirement on the land lease the house sat on. She would allow herself that full time to hibernate, build that cocoon she was hoping would lead to her metamorphosis. Lick her wounds. Restore herself in some small way. And then she would figure out what she was going to do.

If she could get her books published and make a little bit of money off them, maybe she would be able to stay on the Cape and not return to the world of accounting. She had loved accounting and the preciseness of it until the shame of having her husband lose all their money behind her back ruined her love for the trade.

But getting books published when you had little confidence in yourself was more than challenging. She had been querying agents off and on for a while now. Even with all her projects yet to be completed. Rachel's critique group had been effusive enough in their praises that she had been able to ignore Todd's comments long enough to send out queries from time to time. None had yet requested a full manuscript from her, so she hadn't ever actually completed any of her many projects. But now she was more determined than ever. She would prove to herself that she could finish one at least. Even if it never saw the light of a bookstore. Rachel would have that accomplishment to be proud of. It would make this odd time of hiding worthwhile.

Wiping the tears from her face, Rachel pushed up from the couch. She couldn't allow Jake Callaghan to affect her in any way. She was a grown woman, even if a little damaged. No one else's thoughts about her mattered except her own. Only she was allowed to think she was a failure. And she was trying to get away from that type of less than helpful thought.

Squaring her shoulders, Rachel marched over to her laptop and pulled up her current document. If she was going to suffer through feelings, she might as well channel them usefully into some angst for her heroine. That was one of the only positive things she could seem to find about all that she had been through in the past couple of years. She definitely was no stranger to the depths of despair. She would know how to accurately describe the thoughts and sensations as she wrote the dark moments in her books. Of course, since she was writing romantic fiction, she'd be sure to get it all resolved and tied up with a happily ever after at the end. Too bad she couldn't figure out to write that chapter for herself.

Giving her head a shake, Rachel admonished herself for the negative thoughts. While she wasn't yet ready for her end to be close, she was determined to write some happier chapters on the pages of her book of life. Starting with her viewpoint.

She had survived her first encounter with Jake Callaghan. Neither of them had combusted. She wouldn't have minded entirely if he had done so, she thought with a small smile. But that would be a waste of all that rugged handsomeness, she acknowledged, proud of herself for being able to see past her hurts to the bald facts.

Jake Callaghan was a ridiculously handsome man. Ridiculous because it was wasted on such a poor specimen. But then how was she to know? She was a different person than she had once been. Not for the better in all ways, but definitely different. Perhaps Jake had grown and changed. These things do happen. Even though at nineteen he was nearly a man, he was still a high school student the last time she saw him. She should allow that he might not be so dreadful.

Not that she was expecting herself to try to be friends with him. But if she was going to strive to acknowledge and forgive herself for past wrongs, perhaps she should figure out a way to do the same of Jake and his friends. Nearly a lifetime had passed since all that had taken place. It was time for her to move on.

With her determination firmly in place, Rachel's fingers flew over the keyboard, producing a surprising number of words for her daily word count tracker and when she read them over to make sure she hadn't gone too far astray from her rough outline, she was pleased to see that it wasn't drivel. In fact, a normal person would probably think they were pretty good.

But the former valedictorian who married someone who undermined her confidence had no way of knowing whether or not she was doing well. Rachel decided to count the day as a win. She had passed an emotional hurdle that needed to be faced without falling apart, she had finished the painting of the plaster she had repaired in one room, trim and all, and she had gotten quite a chunk written on her novel. And it wasn't even dark out yet.

She would take the win and hug it to herself. Perhaps she ought to get one of those star charts people got for little kids' accomplishments. It would feel good to see her stars marching along the chart. The thought brought a smile to her face. Now that she was no longer terrified of running into anyone, maybe she could actually go to the store and buy it.

Rachel decided to cook up one of her favorite easy meals as her personal reward for the day and then curled up in front of a good romcom to laugh away her worries.

The next morning, when she checked her inbox, there was a message from one of the agents she had queried, and she nearly had heart failure.

Dear Ms. Whitney,

I enjoyed the sample you sent and am intrigued enough to want to read more. Please send the entire manuscript following the guidelines on our website at your earliest convenience. I look forward to reading the rest of your work.

Regards,

Pauline Chorniak

After staring at her computer screen in shock for the beat of several minutes or perhaps hours or maybe just a heartbeat, Rachel squealed, jumping up to dance around the room before reality sank in. She didn't have that particular manuscript finished. She didn't have any manuscripts completed. She should never have jumped the gun and started querying when she wasn't actually ready. The euphoria quickly dissipated. She couldn't send incomplete work. And what if the agent lost interest in the time it took her to complete the work?

Taking deep, calming breaths and muttering words of encouragement to herself, Rachel opened her spreadsheet where she kept track of who she had sent what just to double check which manuscript she had queried Ms. Chorniak with.

Historical Romance Novel #3 – sent 3 months ago.

Ok. The agent took three months to respond so she shouldn't very well expect Rachel to reply the absolute second she received the invitation to submit. From what she had read in various online groups, it is much better to submit a polished work after a bit of a delay than to send rubbish right away.

Rachel glanced toward the stairs. Renovations could wait. She would work through her manuscript right away. Maybe she could do both, complete the manuscript AND send it promptly.

By the end of the week Rachel had barely slept, ate, or showered but for the first time in her life she had completed a full manuscript and was somewhat confident in its fitness to be presented to an agent. Pure joy flooded her being all the way from the top of her head to the tips of her in need of a pedicure toenails. She had accomplished one thing she had set out to do. There was still no guarantee the agent would want to sign her, but in that moment it didn't matter. Rachel had completed a manuscript, something she had begun to fear she could never actually do.

If only Todd were alive to see this. If only Aunt Eileen were alive to see this. They would have vastly divergent reactions. And Rachel's feelings were very different for how she thought they would each react. A part of her childishly wished she could say I told you so to Todd. She HAD in fact finally completed a manuscript. Aunt Eileen would be so proud of her.

It had been her aunt's love of reading that had really fueled her own. Despite Rachel's more academic bent, somehow her aunt's love for those sweet historical romance novels had rubbed off on her charge. The two of them had spent many a pleasurable Saturday afternoon curled up on sofas in the front room devouring those books. The evidence of their love was still strewn about the house on bookshelves in every available wall space.

In the years since Rachel had left the Cape, Aunt Eileen had visited her wherever they agreed to meet. And most of those visits were spent at least a little bit in reading together. Also, in more recent times, after Rachel had started trying to write herself, they had spent half their conversations dissecting her stories and plotting out the twists and turns required to provide the most satisfying endings.

Perhaps that was why Rachel had never been able to finish a manuscript before. She had never truly believed in the happy endings. But now, after losing everything else, it was the only thing left for her to cling to. And she was confident Aunt Eileen would love this one. Hopefully Pauline Chorniak would, too.

She was about to formulate the email to send it off to the agent, but Rachel decided she ought to sleep on it. She very carefully saved her document in the many places the other paranoid authors on the websites assured her were necessary to safeguard against hard drive failure and powered off her laptop. She really ought to eat, shower, and get a good sleep. Tomorrow would be soon enough to send it.

The next morning, all her fears were waiting for her as soon as she opened her eyes. She remembered what had happened to other writers she knew online. What if her laptop had crashed as had happened to Bria? What if the cloud server was fried as had happened to Jenn? What if she hadn't actually saved the correct document? What if she hadn't actually finished the story? What if there were too many plot holes?

What if she just got out of the bed and went and checked?

She hadn't used to be such a neurotic disaster, she was certain. Her childhood had been normal. Idyllic even. Of course, losing both her parents when she was an awkward thirteen-year-old hadn't been the best for her mental or emotional development, but Rachel was well aware that her aunt had gone to great lengths to provide her a stable home. Rachel was pretty sure she had weathered most of the teen years as well as could be expected.

But the torment she had faced at school for being such a young and smart classmate had probably stunted some of her emotional growth, and then Todd's manipulations had just helped her along the uncomfortable path of self-doubt.

That would have to stop.

She had completed a manuscript. Even if the world imploded and the document was nowhere to be found on the multiple places she had stored it, she had proven to herself that it could be done. She, Rachel Whitney, had completed a full-length manuscript of publishable, acceptable length within the industry.

At this point it didn't matter if the agent liked it or if she could find a buyer for it. Rachel was going to bask in the experience of being this proud of herself for a few more minutes.

But then she did rush to her laptop to ensure that it was still working and that her files were all where they were supposed to be. Rachel had to chuckle over the vagaries of believing everyone on the internet. But it certainly didn't hurt to be safer than sorry.

After one more full read through to check for any typos or story holes, she finally composed that email and sent the full manuscript off to the literary agent. At this point, unless she hired an editor of her own, she could no longer see any of the mistakes. She had looked at it far too many times. She was confident it was the best she could make of it at that time. And she was proud of that little story.

Not so little, really, as it had settled in at just under one hundred thousand words once she was finished editing. She felt confident it was a good length. But was willing to be told otherwise by an agent or editor, she thought with a smile, feeling excited and optimistic for the first time in ages.

Suddenly she was filled with a desire to go for a run. She hadn't run or really done much exercise of any sort since she participated in track and field in high school. Rachel had complicated feelings about her experience on the track team. She had thrived in the camaraderie of being on a team and had thought she was an asset to them, but when they hadn't won gold as they'd expected, there were some eyes and fingers pointing at her as the smallest and likely the weakest member of the team.

In hindsight, which was always clearest, Rachel knew it was her own insecurities that had made her think that. Or perhaps some of her teammates had actually thought she was a problem. But when observed objectively, she knew she had some of the best times despite her smaller stature. But the experience had made her quit the team and quit sports altogether. She hadn't run since except to catch a bus.

But now she felt the urge. And wanted to follow through on the impulse.

She didn't know if she even owned a pair of running shoes anymore, but she suspected there might be some of Eileen's lying about. A quick search revealed multiple pairs that would fit her.

Within moments she was laced up and stretching her quads and hams. It had been so long, she wasn't sure if she was even doing it right, but the well of optimism filling her needed an outlet, and she had no desire to ignore it.

Rachel tried to keep herself to a slow and steady pace. She had no desire for an injury her first time back out in so many years. Running on the beach would be a protection for her bones but would make her muscles have to work a little harder. Finally finding a stride that seemed comfortable but she knew she would feel later, Rachel allowed herself to bask in the good feelings.

As she jogged and her breathing deepened, Rachel's mind drifted to the other encounters she'd had the week previous. Tina and Angela. Rachel was surprised to find out just how many of her former classmates had remained on the small island. They had lost touch when Rachel left the island. The only person she had remained in contact with was Aunt Eileen.

But seeing those two girls, women now, she supposed, had been a reminder that her time on Cape Avalon hadn't been all bad. Rachel wasn't sure if they could be friends again after all the time that had flowed under the bridge, but it wasn't as though there was a great crowd of candidates for the position of Rachel Whitney's friend, so maybe she would consider it.

Rachel was in the grocery store staring at the wine selections when Angela had approached her.

"Go for the Moscato, that's always the right choice," she had said with a wide, friendly grin before her eyes had widened with pleased surprise. "Rachel? Is that you? Oh, my stars! I would recognize you anywhere. You've barely changed a bit, you lucky thing."

That had surprised a laugh out of Rachel. "You are being kind," she had said while she wracked her brain trying to identify the woman. Then she too had widened eyes as she asked, "Angela?"

"Yes," Angela had nearly shouted as she grinned at Rachel. "Three children later, I don't look like the high school track star anymore, do I?"

There was no way she could reply to that. Rachel opened her mouth hoping something socially correct would come to mind but all that came out was slightly nervous laughter.

But her old friend didn't seem to mind in the least.

"Are you really here? I can hardly believe it. I haven't seen you since we graduated. I was so sorry to hear about your aunt. She was such a dear."

The lump that had formed in Rachel's throat immediately upon these words had been hard to swallow, but she had managed a wan smile.

"Never mind about sad things, I can't believe you're actually here. You didn't answer, are you here for a bit? Or just to clear out? I would love to spend some time with you, and I know Tina would want to as well. You remember her, right? She moved back six or seven years ago, and we've been tight ever since. Even if you're just here to clear out, we could help if you're too busy to come for a girls' night."

Rachel stared at the offer. Why would her former classmate make it? Sure, they had sort of been friends in high school, but as they had established, that had been a long time ago. She didn't know what to say. Angela laughed again.

"You have been gone from the island too long, and now I've made you uncomfortable, haven't I? You've forgotten that there are people who just offer to help for no reason. That's ok, sweetie. You'll get back to that if you stay long enough. And it wasn't for no reason. There aren't enough lovely people here. Tina and I were just talking about the good times we had with you back in the day not that long ago. Do say you'll find the time to spend with us before you leave."

There was no resisting that appeal. "I'm not actually completely sure how long I'm here for, but I am trying to fulfill the residency requirement."

"No way! That's awesome."

The other woman's enthusiasm was gratifying.

"So when can we hang out? You'd better get a second bottle," she added with a laugh and a nod at Rachel's basket of groceries before chagrin filled her face. "No, that's not right. I ought to be showing you hospitality, not the other way around. I was just so thrilled at the idea of adult conversation that my brain got lost along the way."

Rachel hadn't felt this light in ages. All she did was laugh in Angela's presence. Very little conversation was required on her part. She didn't remember her being quite that much of a motor-mouth in high school, but that might have been because they had all been too busy talking over one another. Now Rachel didn't feel as though she had much to say. But she was thrilled at the prospect of listening.

After quick introductions when Angela's three children had arrived, the two women had exchanged phone numbers with Angela promising to coordinate with Tina as to available dates. Rachel had even found herself offering her own flexibility.

Now, jogging along the beach, Rachel was still surprised at her eagerness to have a girls' night. She barely even knew what that was. She and Todd had been practically attached at the hip since she was seventeen. At first, she had loved it and hadn't minded the lack of female companionship, but then she had begun to feel isolated and missed the unique interaction of girlfriends.

Those thoughts were unhelpful, Rachel insisted to herself. It was all in the past now and didn't matter. She was going to have girlfriends now, if she stayed on the Cape, and if she wanted them.

Rachel reminded herself as she enjoyed the steady rhythm of her feet hitting the hard sand that she was an independent, grown woman now. She didn't have to do anything she didn't want to do. If she spent time with her former friends and didn't enjoy it, she didn't have to repeat it. But her heart quickened at the thought. She knew she was going to love it.

She had forgotten how much fun hanging out with girlfriends could be. When she had thought longingly of them over the last decade, she had attributed it to being so young, but her few minutes of interaction with Angela in the busy grocery store had made her think it was the unique woman, not their age when they'd been friends. Or perhaps just female friendships in general.

With a shake of her head, Rachel pushed through the challenging feelings that welled up within her and concentrated on keeping her breathing and pace steady. It wouldn't due to overexert herself just because she was trying to outrun complicated feelings.

Yes, she had stunted herself with her rash decisions so long ago, and, yes, she only had herself to blame. But she wasn't an old crone just yet. There was still plenty of life ahead of her. At thirty-three, while it was quite late to be figuring out life, there was still time. Even for children, possibly, she thought with a pang as she remembered the clamor when Angela's two daughters and adorable son had interrupted their conversation.

They appeared to be pleasant children. They hadn't interrupted on purpose. They were just far too excited about whatever had been on their minds. Rachel hadn't minded in the least. She had been glad, really. She needed to process her thoughts and feelings about rekindling old friendships before she got too deeply into it, anyway.

But they had seemed like a beautiful little family. And a pang of jealousy twisted through Rachel for a brief beat before she released the negative thought. Rachel reminded herself that she was happy for Angela. Truly happy. Suddenly she remembered

Angela's determination for children back in high school. They had been friends despite their very different life plans.

In a certain way, it would seem they had both achieved what they'd set out to do. Rachel's lips twisted. She could only hope Tina's dreams had turned out to be exactly as she had hoped. She wondered if Tina had managed to become a veterinarian. And if Angela had ended up marrying the quarterback she'd had her heart set on their senior year.

Rachel hadn't asked any questions, too surprised by the encounter for her brain to catch up. She would remedy that when they met again.

The lighthouse came into view and Rachel continued toward it, intrigued by the sight in the water. It looked as though the water was churning. She hadn't checked her timetable, but since she couldn't see the rocks that were normally sticking up out of the water, the tide must be in. But how odd that the waves seemed to be competing with one another. The turmoil matched what Rachel envisioned going on inside her mind and she loved the outward visualization.

It was just like the pier that she ought to be rebuilding in front of her house. One more symbol of her life. Rachel suddenly grinned. She wondered if all authors thought in metaphors like that or if she was just a weirdo.

Her mouth was beginning to dry out and she regretted the impulse that made her leave without grabbing a water bottle. Rookie mistake. She shook her head but then shrugged. It hadn't been that far or that long. And in the early winter coolness, it wasn't likely she was nearing dehydration. She would just remember for next time.

Her feet were even lighter on the return trip, which was almost unfathomable. How could a few positive encounters make her feel like a different person? It must be the ions in the seaside air, she surmised with another smile that felt almost unfamiliar on her face.

If only Aunt Eileen were there to see it.

But if she were, would Rachel even be there? Rachel had stuck with her vow until Eileen was no longer there to witness her change of heart. Not that this had ever been Rachel's intention. She hadn't been running away from her beloved aunt. It was just her humiliation and inner turmoil that caused her to make such a rash decision.

And then her subsequent decisions had made her ashamed to retract the first ones.

But now that was all behind her, Rachel reminded herself. She was a novelist now. With a house that was paid off and a very small nest-egg. Since she was such a well-educated accountant and there was no longer anyone who could possibly sabotage her efforts, surely she could make that nest egg last. Maybe even make it grow if she was frugal enough.

Nearing her own house, Rachel slowed her pace, bringing her breathing and heartbeat back to normal, and took a moment to enjoy the view as she looked out over the ever moving Atlantic Ocean. The vastness of it made her feel small but mighty. In all that huge vastness, her problems seemed puny by comparison. And easily washed away or set to rights. She had nothing to worry about or be ashamed of. She was an accomplished woman who had made it this far without killing anyone or committing any crimes, she reminded herself with a wry attempt at humor. Sure, she'd made mistakes, but so had everyone.

Today was a new day.

Chapter Eleven

T
he wait to hear back from the agent was killing her!

All her resolutions to look at the bright side were being threatened by the interminable wait. But Rachel was determined to make the needed effort. She dutifully researched other agents she thought might be a good fit. Even ones who she had already queried with a different work. She now had a completed manuscript. This gave her even more confidence to submit.

She also workshopped her blurb, getting feedback from other authors as well as her query letter. She set the goal of querying one agent each day. That wasn't so very many when one considered the sheer number of players in the crowded market. But good agents in her genre were limited, so she continued to research and query. Determination filled her, but it ebbed and flowed as she waited to hear back.

There had also been two requests for partial submissions that week. Those had helped to keep her positive. But she was glad for the distraction of going to visit with friends.

Or she hoped they were to be friends. Hope again surged within her, but Rachel tried to keep it within reasonable bounds. If she didn't allow her hopes to be too high then the disappointment might not be too terrible if it didn't work out as she hoped.

That had been a life philosophy her parents had used to preach to her and one that had served her well after their deaths. Especially when she had moved in with Aunt Eileen. She had been terrified during that long last drive to the Cape from their apartment in New York. Or so it had seemed long. Now as an adult, Rachel knew it would have been at most five or six hours, unlike her much longer drive from Chicago a couple weeks previous. But she had spent the entirety of that first drive telling herself not to have her hopes up. In that case, it had worked spectacularly.

Living with her aunt had been a privilege and a joy. The only thing that would have been better would have been if her parents had never died. But that was a fruitless wish.

Eileen had often lamented that she was a single woman and worried that she wouldn't be able to provide sufficiently well-rounded parenting for Rachel. Perhaps that was why she never rebuked Rachel for her determination to remain far from the island after high school.

She could never ask her now.

Rachel admonished herself for allowing her thoughts to stray in this direction and turned her thoughts to something more practical and productive – her appearance. She fidgeted with her hair and frowned over the wayward strands. It was the one downside of living right on the shore, her hair often resisted her efforts at keeping it tame.

After grabbing the bottle of wine from the fridge that Angela had advised her to get and that she had never gotten around to drinking by herself, Rachel glanced around the main floor of her house before she went out the door. Everything was in its place. Almost how Aunt Eileen would have had it, with a few exceptions to accommodate for Rachel's slightly different taste. Her aunt hadn't minded fussy things. Perhaps she even loved them. It was the one thing she didn't admire about her aunt. Rachel couldn't abide knickknacks. They seemed like just one more thing that needed to be kept cleaned and dusted.

After having admired Evelyn's house, Rachel knew she didn't mind them as much as she thought she had. Her neighbor seemed to love trinkets almost as much as Eileen had. But Evelyn's seemed, at least, to stick to a theme of some sort, not like Aunt Eileen's, which had just been a hodgepodge of things she had collected through the years.

On the other hand, Rachel loved the history of Aunt Eileen's eclectic collection. There were stories there. But it was still too much for her esthetic. She had boxed up most of the odds and ends and they were currently in the attic. Maybe one day she would be able to part with them. For now, she would hold onto them as one last connection to her aunt.

Rachel blew a frustrated puff of air toward the stray hair that was tickling her cheek. She didn't need such random thoughts sabotaging her evening. A girls' night. She didn't think she had ever partaken in such a mysterious event. Unless you counted sleepovers when she was a kid.

If a girls' night was anything like a sleepover, Rachel was looking forward to it with a thrill. And if it was awkward, well, at least there would be wine. And she was a grown up. She could drive herself home whenever she felt like it. She wouldn't even be forced into the awkward situation of having to wait for a ride if she suddenly wanted to leave.

She quickly locked the door and rushed to her car. She didn't care if no one else on the island locked their doors. She had grown up in New York for the first thirteen years of her life and then spent most of her adult years in Chicago. No one in a big city would even think of leaving their doors unlocked. It was not a habit that would be easy to break even if Rachel was inclined to do so.

Now that she was living alone for the first time in her life, she had no desire to have unlocked doors whether she was home or not. She had watched too many movies to be comfortable entering the house when she got home in the dark later that evening.

Perhaps she was allowing her imagination to run away on her, she allowed with a grin as she started her car.

The old beater she had driven from Chicago was still running. Just barely. It resisted her efforts to start for a moment but finally the engine caught and she was on her way. The island wasn't all that big; it wouldn't take her long to find Angela's house.

When she pulled up to the address her friend had given her, Rachel's lips pursed into a silent whistle. It might not be right on the beach, but it was a beautiful home. Apparently, Angela and her husband were doing well for themselves.

Rachel shook her head. She ought to know better than to make judgments of that sort. Hadn't she learned anything in her life thus far? One mustn't assume that anything was as it seemed. She was sure people would have thought all sorts of things about her and Todd from looking at their lovely home. Probably none of them would have been true.

That brought genuine amusement to her face that lasted even after she had rung the doorbell. She was nervous but it seemed to be within bounds.

She reminded herself that she had taken self-defense classes. No matter what might take place that evening, there was nothing that could cause permanent damage to her. Rachel recognized this was a rather extreme thought, but if it helped her get over her social anxiety about meeting these old acquaintances, she'd take whatever worked.

That kept her smile in place. She really didn't need to feel fearful about spending the evening with Angela and Tina. Even if her first encounter with Tina had been less than stellar, Angela had seemed thrilled to see her and professed to be very excited about the evening before them. Her own excitement resurged.

When she first walked into Angela's beautiful home, there was a flurry of introductions to her husband as he was ushering the children out the door, as well as a brief tour, and then questions about beverage preferences, and social chitchat. Then they were settled in the large family room with a fire crackling in the wide-mouthed fireplace and the two old friends fell silent, staring at Rachel for an uncomfortable moment.

Or at least it was uncomfortable for Rachel until Tina's face split in a grin.

"I can't believe you're here. This is wonderful. It has been awesome being back here with Angela for the last six years, but having you here with us now is just icing on the cake." She then glanced down at herself with a sheepish smile. "Don't mention cake. I just started another program."

Angela laughed. "Should you be drinking wine, then?"

"Wine isn't as many points," Tina pointed out before turning back to Rachel. "What's your secret? You look like you've barely eaten a meal since you turned thirty. Thirty was my downfall. With my active practice, everything was fine until I hit the big three oh."

Rachel didn't want to talk about anyone's weight, including her own, and she was surprised by the exuberance of Tina's welcome. They had been friendly in high school, not exactly friends, as far as Rachel was concerned. But she wasn't going to split hairs, and she did want to get to know them as adults. "Active practice? I've been dying to know if you managed to become a veterinarian."

"Dying to know, huh?" Tina countered with a teasing wiggle of her eyebrows. "It wouldn't have been the least bit challenging to find out if you'd looked."

Despite her apparent enthusiastic acceptance of Rachel into their little group, it would seem there was a little bitterness over her not having stayed in touch. Rachel realized she would have to share some of herself with these two if she wanted a true chance at being friends. She should have listened to more mindset podcasts on the topic, she thought with a twitch of amusement.

"That's valid, I suppose, but have you kept up with me online?"

"I'm not the one who said I was dying to know something about you."

"Tina, that's enough. You know you're happy to have Rachel here; you even said so. There's no need to be snarky about it now. Just because she's skinny and beautiful is no reason to be hateful."

"I also don't have any kids to show for anything, so there's nothing to be envious about me," Rachel added, knowing both of the women, who obviously weighed more than she did, were profoundly proud of their families.

"There is that," Tina agreed with a grin. "Why didn't you have kids? Too busy being a brainiac?" When Angela made a sound of disapproval, Tina made an apologetic face. "I know, it's probably not PC for one woman to ask another woman that since it's likely there are genuine reasons, but if we're going to be friends, we probably ought to know what those reasons are. Or is it too soon?"

Rachel's stomach clenched before she reminded herself nothing here could hurt her. If anything needed to be done, she could just outrun either of the two women. The funny thought steadied her nerves.

"Yeah, something like that," she finally answered with a shrug. "Brainiacs don't make time for kids."

"Rachel, ignore Tina," Angela interjected with a laugh. "She's just jealous and feeling awkward about it. Now come on, tell us what you're doing with your house. I heard you're renovating."

Rachel sighed. Small town gossip strikes again. But it was the harmless sort. It didn't hurt or matter.

"I'm not making any major changes. It's a wonderful old house for one thing, only a minor facelift is needed. For another, I don't have the resources to make any major changes."

"I thought you were making the big bucks at some big firm in the big city," Tina inserted. Finally, Rachel was fed up with being so accepting of the snidely teasing remarks.

"I thought you went to university so you should at least have picked up a bit more vocabulary."

It was the snarkiest thing she thought she had ever said in her entire adult life, and she was surprised how good it felt in the moment. That must be why people did it. But the good feeling didn't last until both of the other women burst into laughter.

"She's got you there, Tina, doesn't she?"

Tina was actually laughing so hard she had to wipe a tear from her face. "That she does. I didn't know if you were ever going to fight back. You never did back in school."

"No, I should have, though."

"Yes, you should have. And yes, I should have a more varied way of expressing myself. But Angela's right. I'm jealous of your bony little body."

All three women laughed at that, and to Rachel's surprise she sank back into the couch cushions and relaxed slightly. Taking a fortifying sip from her glass, she looked at the other two women.

"To be honest, even if I had the money, I don't think I could change much about the house. It feels like a violation of her memory, you know?"

Angela nodded with understanding and Tina appeared to relax even more into her own seat, as though she had finally accepted Rachel into the dynamic.

"I don't think she would want you to feel that way," Tina pointed out, surprising everyone in the room. Embarrassment tripped across her face but she carried on. "I didn't know her as well as you did, of course, but from what I could tell, she loved you very much. And for that reason, she would want you to be happy, or at least comfortable, in her house. In fact, I'm pretty sure she would want you to think of it as your house now and to do with it whatever you want. I know that's how I would feel if it were my kid and I had passed."

Rachel's eyebrows rose at the other woman's rather convoluted expressions but nodded. She wasn't wrong. She knew in her mind that Aunt Eileen would love what she was doing with the house. And Tina was right that she would absolutely want her to be happy there. But in her heart, it still felt a little wrong even though she wasn't making any major changes.

"You'll have to come and see what I'm doing and give me your opinions. This house is amazing, Angela. Have you lived here long?"

Angela's grin was infectious. "Isn't it awesome? I can't take very much credit. We had a builder. The only thing I did was pick out finishes."

"You made excellent choices," Rachel insisted. Her admiration was genuine. It was a remarkably welcoming space even for all its grandeur.

"Thanks, hun. I can't even tell you how many books and magazines I devoured while the house was being built. I watched every home decoration show in existence as well. We're pretty happy with it but once you're living in a space, there's always something you would change. And then you can't really see it anymore when it just becomes home. So, I do appreciate the compliments, thank you."

Rachel had stiffened slightly at the other woman's endearment. It was too similar to Todd's syrupy sweet "Honey" that always preceded one of his condescending pronouncements. But the rest of Angela's speech restored her to her previously almost comfortable state.

"Ok, ladies, spill," Angela declared after the briefest silence descended amongst them. "Seeing as we haven't seen Rachel since high school, let's say everyone has to give at least the broad strokes description of their lives in the meantime to catch the others up."

Trepidation filled Rachel but the other two women didn't seem to notice as they were too busy laughing and talking over each other to fill Rachel in on the last decades of their lives.

"I went to New York for college but didn't love the program I had chosen. I got an Associate's in Child Psychology but haven't practiced except with my own three," Angela started out. "You met my hunky husband. He was the best thing that came out of my college experience. We married before we even graduated, and our first was in the oven at my graduation. Tyler was from Maine, so he was happy to move south to the Cape, back to my hometown when he graduated. He did the full degree he was aiming for so we lived in the married students' residence with a newborn until he graduated, then we crashed with my parents until we got settled. He invented some computer programs so he was able to work from anywhere with decent internet and as you can see, we're doing ok for ourselves even without me pulling in a paycheck. I thought about going to work when our youngest started school, but I don't hate being a woman of leisure, so we decided it was ok for me to stay home."

Rachel looked around the well-appointed home from what she could see from where she was sitting. "Unless you have maids and nannies, it doesn't really look to me like you're a woman of leisure," she commented, causing Tina to nod in approval.

"There's the right attitude of support from a friend."

Rachel flushed from the compliment.

Angela laughed and shrugged. "Well, more leisure than if I was working in addition."

Tina waved away her friend's conversation and added her own update. "I went away to school, got my science degree and then veterinary school. I've been back on the Cape for six years. I worked with a veterinarian in Florida for a couple years after school to gain some experience before I came here and opened my own clinic."

"Do you enjoy being in business for yourself?"

Tina shrugged and nodded at the same time as though undecided. "There are parts I love, like the fact that if it's quiet, I can close up and go to the beach. But I don't love the business-y things, like I have to either hire an administrator or do it myself. The island isn't that big, so there aren't an overwhelming number of pets. And it's only pets, nothing truly challenging."

"Have you thought of leaving?"

"I've thought of it but so far I've dismissed the thought, since there is more to hold me here than draw me away. My kiddo loves it here, and my parents are thrilled to have us."

"That must be so nice for all of you," Rachel murmured, hoping to sound supportive rather than jealous.

Tina grinned. "That sounded quite sincere. Good job."

Rachel laughed but didn't say anything more.

"Your turn now, Rach," Tina called making Rachel smile wider. She hadn't been called Rach since her school days. While it sounded a little awful on one hand, on the other, she loved that someone felt comfortable enough to shorten her name.

But now it was her turn. Should she bare her soul or give the short story? They'd known each other since childhood but this was a fun girls' night, no need to make it too heavy.

"Well, as you know, I left right after we graduated. I went up to Boston early and got settled into my dorm. I loved school so decided to stay longer than necessary." She laughed along with the others as Tina shook her head and called her a brainiac again. "So, if you can believe that anyone would want this, I have my Masters in Forensic Accounting. I married my college sweetheart and we settled in Chicago, which is where he was from. It was very cold there, but we travelled a fair bit to escape. He was killed almost two months ago. So, I settled everything there and came here to regroup."

The two other women were staring at her with almost equal expressions of amazement and discomfort, as though they had a million questions but weren't sure if they should ask them. Given the active gossip network, Rachel was certain the sensational news of her husband's death would have been spread around the island. But she doubted they would ask her for details. Or rather she hoped they wouldn't. Not on their first time together.

Tina forced a laugh. "You're right. Who in their right mind would want a master's degree in accounting?"

Rachel giggled. She actually giggled. It was the lightest sound that had emerged from her body since she was a teenager. And it felt heavenly. The prickly Tina had made her giggle. Life was good on the Cape, she decided with a smile.

"I might not have been in my right mind, but I loved studying it. And practicing it. It often felt like a treasure hunt."

"Will you do that here?" Angela asked with a slight frown. "While I'm sure accountants are always needed, forensic accounting seems more specialized than the sorts of clients you might find here."

"And I'm pretty sure there are already several accountants here," Rachel added, agreeing with Angela's assessment. "I wasn't planning on trying my hand at opening an office here. If I decide to stay, I am hoping to do some freelancing work."

"So, you don't intend to join Angela as a woman of leisure?"

Rachel shook her head. "For all our education, my husband and I made some flawed decisions along the way. I don't have the luxury of that choice. But I do have a space of time within which I can figure things out."

"What sort of things?" Her new friends were curious.

Rachel smiled and lifted her shoulders a little helplessly. "What to do with my life, I suppose."

Angela wrinkled her nose. "Aren't you supposed to know that part already? You're a little young for a mid-life crisis, aren't you?"

Rachel laughed. "I've always been ahead of the curve, haven't I?"

"I suppose you have, but what do you mean? I thought you loved maths, so your work as a forensic accountant sounds perfect for you."

Rachel sighed. She wasn't going to get away with avoiding the hardest topic. She wondered if it would make them friends or strangers. She took a deep breath and kept it to the barest bones of the story.

"I loved university life as much as I always knew I would. I met Todd soon after I arrived at the school and we became fast friends. We had much in common and I loved him very much. But I was also very young and immature in many ways. I'm not sure if Todd loved me as much as I thought he did, even at first. But for certain not at the end. We had troubles. That led me to not asking all the questions I ought to have about what he was doing with his time. It turned out that he had developed an addiction to gambling and his debts added up to a considerable amount. It's quite shameful for a forensic accountant to end up penniless because she didn't keep an eye on her accounts."

"Oh no, Rachel, sweetie, I'm so sorry." Ever tender-hearted, Angela's sympathy was instantaneous. Even the much more hardened Tina appeared shaken by Rachel's story. But Rachel didn't want either of them feeling sorry for her. She shrugged, even if she wasn't really as careless as she would like them to think.

"This is why I need to figure out what I'm going to do with my life."

"So, you think you can't do your work because of one mistake?" Tina scoffed at her.

"Would you trust me with your money knowing I couldn't keep track of my own?"

"Everyone's entitled to one mistake," Tina insisted.

"What if that one mistake was your money?" Rachel insisted right back. They stared at one another belligerently. Then Tina laughed.

"I can see that you truly believe you are no longer worthy to count other people's money. But that in itself proves to me that you would never make that same mistake with someone else's money. Never mind about that, though. I believe that if you really loved that job, you wouldn't allow this to take it away. So, what are you thinking of doing instead?"

"Becoming a writer."

Rachel said it defiantly and there was a beat of silence before her two friends laughed. Rachel smiled, completely understanding. Everyone claimed they wanted to write a book, very few people ever actually did it.

"Have you published anything yet?"

Rachel shook her head. "My husband's lack of enthusiasm made me struggle, so I haven't yet gotten very far. But I've had a request from an agent."

"Oh, how exciting," Angela enthused. "I know some people talk about writing a book one day, but I can barely compose a letter to family let alone write a full chapter of anything. How do you keep the story straight?"

Rachel laughed, delighted with the supportive question and proceeded to tell them a little bit of her ideas, knowing instinctively that no one would be as enthused about her stories as she and her aunt had been, but still excited to share anyway.

Chapter Twelve

The visit with her old friends the night before had done something to restore a little of Rachel's self-respect or self-worth or whatever a psychologist might call it. She awoke with a feeling of calm and contentment that had been missing for a long time.

Rachel examined the feelings she was experiencing as she awakened to a new day with a slight frown. She ought to have been able to find this sense of contentment within herself, not needing external validation to feel good about herself. She smoothed out her frown as she admonished herself. No one, especially not a woman, could exist in a vacuum. Everyone needed other people in their lives to feel truly content. Humans were gregarious creatures. Even introverts needed some sort of contact with others. She shouldn't feel badly that it was only after gaining some friends that she started feeling better. Because, in fact, she had already started to feel better. The girls' night had just solidified that improved sense of well-being.

With a nod and a grin, she sat up in bed and leaned over to grab her laptop. It was time to get in her required words.

Rachel was thrilled that her writing was becoming an easier part of her day. She would have to start giving more thought to the other aspects of a writer's life, but maybe she would leave that until she felt the house was in a state that she could leave off thinking about it.

Today she was going to take the kitchen cupboards apart in order to paint them. It was going to be an invasive task, she was sure. The kitchen was always the center of the house. But that wasn't reason enough to keep putting it off.

Eileen had talked about painting the kitchen for years. She would be so excited if she were there to see it. Rachel kept telling herself that all morning as she worked. First, she had taken everything out of the cupboards and carefully sorted through the items. Any mismatched plasticware was thrown out immediately despite the flutter of disquiet that caused in her midsection. She couldn't be sentimental about old margarine containers, she reminded herself with a forced laugh. And nobody needed outdated takeout menus or long fulfilled shopping lists. Eileen had lived in Sandpiper Cottage for almost forty years. Things had accumulated despite her best efforts not to be a hoarder.

Rachel kept telling herself that it couldn't be a fresh start with clutter in it. And she believed that, for the most part. But it was hard to get rid of anything she knew her aunt had loved. So, she came up with a new tactic. Anything she wasn't yet prepared to part with but which she would classify as "clutter" got put into a box destined for the attic. She could deal with it some other day, but it wouldn't hold up this project nor would it sidetrack her emotionally.

Proud of herself, by the end of the day Rachel had the entire kitchen dismantled, rearranged, sorted, and was already starting to sand the doors she had removed in preparation for the special paint they had insisted was required when she asked for assistance at the hardware store.

It was going to be a big job, but Rachel was satisfied with the progress she had made already in one day.

A glance out the window told her the beach was calling and she had done enough for one day. Rachel quickly cleaned up enough of her mess to be able to consider the house still a home, threw her hair into a ponytail, grabbed her running shoes, and set out on a brisk walk.

As she passed Evelyn's house, it crossed Rachel's mind that she had never taken the neighbor up on her offer to help aside from Evelyn's involving Jake in her house situation. She would have to talk to her soon, but she wasn't sure what she could say to the other woman. She ought to thank her for trying to help, but Rachel wasn't sure how to choke out such a phrase. Perhaps a few more days would help.

As always, the sound and sights of the surf as well as the brisk breeze did their job and left Rachel's mind fresh. The return trip back to the house reminded Rachel of one more thing she needed to think about – the pier.

Should she rebuild it this year?

She hated to admit it, but Jake had a good point when he pointed out the ravages of the weather on the shoreline. Even as she walked the beach, she could see where there had been damage to some properties due to the beach washing away. While she didn't really feel nature ought to be controlled completely, she didn't want to lose her house. Not after she just got there, and especially not if she decided she wanted to stay. But could she just leave it for one more season? It was a risk she would have to calculate. Not that she really had enough factors to be able to do so accurately.

Jake hadn't yet sent her his estimate. Not that she was anxiously awaiting his message. In fact, she told herself, she didn't want to hear from him at all. But she did need to know what it would cost to repair before she could make an informed decision.

Hers was the only property that didn't have a new pier, she realized as she looked up and down the beach. In a way that was reassuring. The shoreline was ninety-nine percent protected. But she also didn't want to be the eyesore of the coast for her neighbors.

She would discuss it with Evelyn, she resolved. It was the thing she missed the most about losing both Eileen and Todd. For all their challenges, Rachel and Todd had always discussed things together. Or so she had thought, anyway. She discussed things with Todd, she rephrased it in her head. Rachel hadn't made an independent decision, really in her entire life. The only one she had ever made was the one that included her vow to never return to Cape Avalon, and that hadn't turned out for the best.

So, she needed a sounding board for the rest of her decisions connected to the house. Rachel wished she had Evelyn's number so she could just call or text her with the invitation to come over and discuss the house, but instead she had to go knock on the door.

"Rachel, how lovely to see you, won't you come in?"

Evelyn's greetings were always so welcoming.

"No, I'm just on my way home from a walk and I realized I don't have your number, so I stopped in to see if you would have time to come over for a coffee tomorrow morning. I had some house things I'd like your opinion on."

"I would love to!" Evelyn answered immediately. "Do you want me to come now? I could come now, if you want? Or what time did you want me?"

Rachel laughed at the other woman's eagerness until she realized it was sincere and then her heart went out to the other woman. She shouldn't be quite that available.

"I wouldn't want to interrupt your evening," Rachel protested. "Any time mid-morning tomorrow would be terrific. I'll need a second cup then," she added with a grin that the other woman returned.

"I'll be there," Evelyn promised, and Rachel left with a wave.

Rachel wondered why she never saw the other woman's husband even though they were neighbors. She had seen the lights of his car arriving home after dark on occasion so she knew he existed, but it didn't seem like he spent much time at his own home. Even on the weekends he seemed to be gone from dawn to dark. She figured there were problems there but knew it wasn't her place to make a judgment. She knew from first-hand experience that there was nothing to be accomplished by speculating about someone else's marriage.

But she would try to be a better friend to her neighbor than she had done thus far. Now that she felt a little more settled within her own circumstances, she was a little better set to help someone else.

That resolution followed her into the next morning. She had again woken up with the birds and gotten in her writing. More words than she usually accomplished, so it started her day off with a sense of empowerment that had been long absent and kept a bright smile on her face throughout the morning. She was also making progress with the sanding, so she felt bright and friendly when there was a soft tap on her back door.

"I baked some muffins. I wasn't sure if you were gluten free or anything like that, but I thought I'd take a chance. Eileen never mentioned it, but you never know these days."

Rachel grinned and her mouth watered slightly as she caught a whiff of the tantalizing smell of freshly baked muffins.

"I would love some glutenous muffins, thank you so much for the kindness. Come in and find a clean spot to make yourself comfortable. Your timing is perfect, as I was just thinking I could use a break." Rachel glanced around before adding. "On second thought, I'm not sure if you'll be able to find anywhere on this floor that is dust free. Why don't you go on through to the porch and I'll bring the coffees out?"

"Don't be silly," Evelyn exclaimed. "I don't mind a bit of dust. I'll just stay with you until we can both go out together."

Rachel appreciated the offer as the friendly gesture it was surely meant to be and she made quick work of making the coffee. Within minutes she had a tray arranged and they made their way out to the wide veranda facing the surf. A glance at the shore told Rachel it was a gentle day. The constant waves were a soft, gentle, background music to their conversation.

"This is lovely," Evelyn commented as she looked around with approval. "You haven't made any changes out here aside from a good scrub, it looks like."

Rachel nodded. "There was nothing wrong out here, in my opinion. I don't have a strong desire to make any massive changes to the house. Mostly just a small facelift. Especially in the kitchen. It's such a messy job, but redoing the cupboards will make a big difference in making it a bright and airy space, more in keeping with the rest of the house."

"Evelyn would love it, I'm sure."

"Thank you for saying so," Rachel murmured, ordering herself not to turn into a watering pot as the other woman's words touched an emotional spot for her. Clearing her throat and taking a sip from her steaming mug helped her get herself together. The breeze made her shiver and gave her a new topic.

"Perhaps coming out here wasn't the best idea. I'm not sure we're far enough south for porch sitting this time of the year."

"It's always a good time for porch sitting," Evelyn countered with a light laugh. "And your view is even more spectacular than mine, I don't mind enjoying it for a bit, especially with a warm cup in my hands."

Rachel nodded in agreement. She would never tire of the setting. It was hard to believe she had voluntarily absented herself from this beauty for so long. She gave her head a shake to dispel the less helpful thought.

"I wanted to ask your opinion and apologize all at the same time." Rachel turned the subject briskly, causing Evelyn to frown.

"What on earth do you have to apologize for?"

"Every other house on our stretch of beach has a lovely deck or wharf or pier stretching out into the ocean. I only have the carcass of what used to be there," Rachel explained as she glanced out at the remnants of the rickety wharf she remembered from her youth.

Evelyn laughed. "Eileen called it a carcass, too. I suppose it does kind of look like old bones sticking up out of the water."

Rachel smiled with the woman.

"But I still don't understand why you're apologizing. You've just taken possession of this house. You weren't even here for years."

"That's just it. I shouldn't have allowed my aunt to let her house and property go like this. She clearly needed help, and I wasn't providing it."

"Eileen was far from destitute or incapable, Rachel," Evelyn admonished gently, surprising Rachel with her candor despite how nervous she always seemed. "This wasn't your doing, I promise you."

"Perhaps not up until I got here, but now it is my problem, and I'm not sure if I'm going to get it resolved."

Evelyn surprised Rachel further by not commenting, merely lifting her eyebrows in question, prompting Rachel into further speech.

"I don't know if I'm going to get it fixed this year. That's what I wanted to talk to you about. Do you think there's a chance our properties might wash away if I don't do anything with it right away?"

"I don't think so, but I'm far from an expert. What good do you think waiting might do, though?"

Rachel shrugged but knew a sheepish expression was on her face. "It will allow me time to decide if I'm staying or not. If I'm not staying, I could leave the responsibility to the next people. If I am staying, I could postpone the expense until I'm a bit more settled."

To Rachel's surprise, the other woman chewed on her lip and look undecided. It almost made her laugh. Rachel realized she had expected the always cheerful woman to instantly agree that Rachel ought to wait on the likely expensive project. She still hadn't heard from Jake with a quote. She had no way of knowing how long these things normally took, but she had thought it would be sooner. Not that she really wanted to hear from him, she assured herself. She just wanted the information in order to be able to decide for herself. But she also really wanted to put the project off indefinitely. And she had wanted Evelyn's support on that, she realized now.

"I don't really think it would make a huge difference to the properties if you don't do the repairs instantly," Evelyn finally said. "As you can see, your pier is pretty much completely gone and has been like that for a while, so it shouldn't make a huge difference. But on the other hand, it might be better sooner rather than later. So, you ought to decide as soon as possible whether or not you intend to stay. I do think the expense might be one of those things that you would recoup in the event of selling. Like you know how those renovation shows say that updating a bathroom will make you back all the money but not updating a bedroom?" When Rachel nodded, Evelyn added, "I think probably you would be able to get extra for the house if the pier is already done, so it doesn't really matter if you spend it or not. Unless you really don't have the money, it might not be worth going into debt for it," she finally concluded with a sheepish expression. "I'm not really being of any help, am I?"

"You actually are," Rachel assured her. "I need someone to discuss it with. I'm not used to being solo. I've never had to decide anything on my own before."

Evelyn's face flooded with sympathy. "I'm so sorry, Rachel, I keep forgetting that you're actually deep in mourning. Your aunt never said much about your husband, so I tend to forget about him, and since Eileen has been gone for six months, it's not so fresh."

"It's probably more fresh for me, since I wasn't here to see that she's gone," Rachel added as tears prickled behind her eyes, but she tried to blink them away. She waved a hand in front of her face. "I'm actually doing mostly fine. But yeah, decisions. I have never been really great at them. I've always had someone to sound things off of."

"Well, sound away," Evelyn exclaimed. "I would love to help you in any way I can. You must realize I have nothing else to do."

Rachel frowned. "Not really, I don't know all that much about you, actually." She held up the coffee pot. "Would you like a refill?"

"If I'm not keeping you from anything," Evelyn returned.

"I'm not in a huge rush to get back to sanding, I can assure you."

Evelyn laughed and held out her cup.

"So, tell me about Evelyn," Rachel said gently as they both huddled over their warm mugs.

"I would give anything to be a mother." Evelyn said the words in a rush as though they had been held back with a great effort.

Rachel nodded. "I can see that you would make a great mom. You'd be the cool mom with the awesome cookies at all the bake sales."

Evelyn's laugh sounded a little watery, but she didn't give way to the tears that were clearly threatening.

"We've tried everything. But I can't keep a pregnancy."

"I'm so sorry, that must be terribly painful." Rachel had been right. You never know what pain is behind someone else's door.

Evelyn nodded as though it was an understatement. "My husband doesn't want to try anymore. It was really expensive. But we've agreed to try one more time, after I've taken six months to do nothing. In case it's stress or something that keeps interfering."

Rachel watched her new friend questioningly. "Is it less stressful to sit at home and stew about it?"

106

Evelyn laughed, but it sounded forced. "Not in the least. But Eric doesn't see it that way. The doctor suggested it, so Eric insisted. If we were going to try again, this was the plan."

"What would you rather be doing?"

Evelyn shrugged. "Anything, really. Doing nothing just leaves me too much time to fret. I can only do so much cleaning. I'll end up washing the paint right off the walls if I'm not careful."

Chapter Thirteen

Rachel laughed as she was sure was Evelyn's intention, but her heart still ached for the other woman. She and Todd had never gotten to the point of wishing or trying for children, but Rachel could understand that it was a very human, very urgent, desire for many women, and she could just imagine that the ache of loss would be immense. A flutter in her midsection that felt almost like empathy made Rachel hesitate. The last thing she needed right now was to have her internal baby clock start ticking just as she had become a widow. She chose to ignore that possibility even as she tried to support her new friend.

Because that was Rachel's new goal. To cultivate a close circle of female friends. She had started the night before by opening her mouth and bleeding all over Angela's beautiful floor with her personal confessions. She had never felt so vulnerable in her life. But for that very reason she could fully appreciate what Evelyn was doing at the moment. And so now they were friends. And Rachel knew instinctively, even though she didn't have a great deal of experience with making and keeping friends, that Evelyn would be a good one.

She reached out and grasped Evelyn's hand.

"Thank you for sharing this with me, Evelyn. I'm sure it must be hard." She swallowed the lump of emotion that had formed in her throat and strove for an upbeat tone. "I would never want you to be washing the paint off your walls, so I will make the sacrifice and allow you to work here, but just as a favor, of course."

That had the desired effect of making Evelyn laugh. Her laughter was a little harder than warranted but Rachel knew it was just the release of pent-up emotions. Evelyn squeezed Rachel's hand that was still in her grasp.

"Thank you, Rachel. I'm so glad you're here. I was so lonely without Eileen. She would be so happy to know we were becoming friends."

This brought the clog of emotion back to Rachel's throat, but she swallowed it back, too. There was no need to turn into a blubbering mess. She had done enough of that. But then she remembered she didn't have to be the buttoned up forensic accountant anymore. If she was going to be a fiction writer, perhaps it would be perfectly acceptable for her to be all up in her emotions. In fact, it might even be considered advisable. Suddenly a gurgle of laughter erupted from deep in her belly, causing Evelyn to look slightly alarmed.

"No, Eve, I'm not losing my mind, or at least, I don't think I am. I have just been going through a lot, as have you, so you can understand that there are more feelings than I can sometimes process at once."

Evelyn smiled. "I can fully relate to that sentiment, but that usually makes me cry not laugh hysterically."

Rachel lifted a shoulder in helplessness. "Don't you think laughter and tears are just two extremes on the same spectrum?"

Evelyn's smile widened. "Are we getting all philosophical now?"

"Nope," Rachel answered quickly and emphatically. "I didn't study a single philosopher and I have no intention of starting now. I wouldn't mind learning a little more about psychology as I don't remember most of what I took in school. But I've always dealt better with the cold hard facts of mathematics than the haziness of philosophy or even psych. But if I'm going to be a successful author, I suppose I'm going to have to learn at least the rudimentaries."

"Are you writing a book?" Evelyn's eyes had rounded in excitement and surprise.

"Did Eileen not tell you? I thought she told you everything."

"Sometimes I wonder if she told me anything," Evelyn grumbled, but there was answering laughter in her voice letting Rachel know she wasn't really offended. "I would think she would have had a hard time keeping that to herself, considering how much she loved to read."

"That was a love she passed on to me, and we spent many an enjoyable hour discussing my stories. But until last week I had never actually finished a book. I have dozens of started projects, though."

"Is that why you're here?" Evelyn asked, her voice tentative as though she didn't really mean to pry.

"You aren't too dumb, are you?" Rachel said without rancor. "It's one of the reasons, yes. I would love to make a go of my writing, and being here could really help."

"Why?"

"Well, it's not over stimulating like in the city. The long walks on the beach are perfect for working out tricky plot points. And the sound of the surf is soothing when I'm feeling like things aren't going so well."

"Will you leave when you're done?" Evelyn's voice was small, as though she was dreading the answer.

Rachel smiled at her new friend and squeezed her hand once more before leaning back in her chair with her mug held tightly in both hands. "I'm not sure if I'll ever be done, to be honest," she finally answered after staring out at the ocean in front of them. "They say once a writer always a writer." She sighed and met Evelyn's gaze squarely. "I had some reasons that I thought were very sincere and important for never returning when I left here when I graduated from high school. And with Aunt Eileen gone, if those reasons continue to bring me pain, there's really no reason for me to stay. Except for the fact that this was the home that I shared with my last living relative, there isn't a great deal holding me here. So, I don't have a strong answer yet as to what I will do. I'm hoping to have the few updates to the house that I want done finished soon so that I can just experience what it is to live here. I do love the beach. I love feeling close to Aunt Eileen here in the house. I love the history and the love that I can feel here. So that is a big draw. Also, the house is paid for, aside from the land lease, which isn't very much, as you know. If I can get over the hurts from the past and make a go of it financially, I would like to stay. I'm just starting to make some friends, including one right next door," she said with a gentle smile at Evelyn, who returned it with a bit of a wobble. "So, I think it would be beneficial for me to see what it feels like to have roots again. But I won't stay if I can't let go of what happened before."

"Do you feel ready to share it with me?"

Rachel sighed again. "The sad part is, as an adult, looking back, it wasn't even that big of a deal. But at the time it hurt me deeply. And then I made my rash vow, which led to later decisions that weren't the best for me. So, it isn't really what happened but how it makes me feel."

Rachel looked at Evelyn and appreciated the very open, understanding expression on her face, as though she were trying very hard to understand but knew she really couldn't. Rachel smiled, took a deep breath, and started her tale with the thought that she was baring her soul more in the last twenty-four hours than she had all together in her entire life.

"I was the smartest kid in my class. I was actually always the smartest kid, so they had me skip a grade in elementary school. This made me be exceptionally young for high school. Some of the other kids resented having basically a child in their class and set out to make it very evident that they didn't appreciate my presence. Not everyone was unpleasant, of course. But there was a boy that I had a crush on. My first crush. He was two years older because he had flunked a grade at some point in his school career. So of course, he had no use for me at all. In hindsight, I think maybe we both suffered from the exact same sentiments – being rather ashamed of being in the same grade. Anyhow, he probably could tell I had a crush on him. Most young girls can't hide such things. And it probably made him feel awkward, but he didn't have the maturity to handle it despite being older. So, he and his friends made it very evident that I was unappealing to them. Mostly with teasing and mockery, especially of my good grades and youthful appearance. And then the teachers chose me as the class valedictorian. My grades called for it, but I was so socially awkward it would probably have been better if they had selected someone else. Anyhow, after four years of teasing and what felt to my young mind as abuse, it culminated in them catcalling and mocking me at our graduation ceremony. I was humiliated, of course. A soon as I had my diploma in hand, I stalked home, packed my bags, and left the island, never to return. Until a couple weeks ago. The stupid thing that hurts me the most now is that they probably never even noticed. The only people I really hurt with my rebellion was me and Aunt Eileen." Tears were leaking down her cheeks by the time she was finished telling Evelyn the sad story.

"Eileen fully understood, I'm sure, sweetie. She never said a single word of complaint about you not visiting. In fact, she often sounded so excited about your adventures whenever you would meet."

"I appreciate you saying that."

"I'm not just saying it," Evelyn replied immediately. "She really loved you and enjoyed spending time with you wherever it was. She even seemed to enjoy the opportunities to leave the island even though she loved it here. If you're beating yourself up over her feelings, I don't think you should. For one thing, you know she was a straight shooter. If it bothered her, surely she would have said something."

Rachel stared at Evelyn feeling tears well up behind her eyes, and she tried to blink them away but at least a couple managed to escape her control. "That is so true about her and not something I thought about in my efforts to beat up on myself. Thank you for the reminder."

They sat in companionable silence for a few moments, each lost in their own thoughts.

"Did she ever mention my husband to you?"

The guilty expression that flitted across Evelyn's face made Rachel laugh. "Why do you look as though you've been caught stealing from the cookie jar?"

Evelyn laughed, too. "Eileen was always quick to defend him and herself whenever she said anything negative about your husband, but it was always evident that she was much less excited about her trip if he was going to be there."

Rachel nodded. She wasn't ready to discuss Todd after her confession session with her friends the night before. But she was glad to note that Eileen had known at least a little about her situation. Rachel wanted to believe her aunt understood and forgave her, but it was hard after all the secrets she had tried to keep. She was appreciating Evelyn's friendship more and more.

"Enough heavy talk for now. Tell me what you think I ought to do about my kitchen."

Evelyn grinned. "You definitely need to tile the wall between the upper and lower cabinets. It will alter the look completely and make cleanup simpler. I also think your countertops need replacing. Other than that, what you're doing with the doors and walls is perfect. Did you pick a color yet?"

"I'm so glad you've asked because the answer is a big fat no. But I have narrowed it down, so I would love your input."

Evelyn actually squealed like a little girl over that. They quickly picked up their mugs and returned to the house giggling and gabbing over paint swatches. Rachel didn't know if she had ever felt so carefree as in that moment. Certainly not since she was thirteen years old and the bottom had dropped out of her life. She was thrilled to be feeling so positive. It had been far too long.

After a while, Evelyn started making sounds about returning to her own house but then she thought of something.

"Did Jake Callaghan stop by? I mentioned your house to him the other day and asked him if he would have room for you. I know you wanted some other names, but he really is the best so I thought if he could squeeze you in, then you wouldn't need anyone else."

Rachel hesitated over how to answer. If Evelyn was friends with Jake, Rachel didn't really want to bad mouth him. But she hadn't decided what to do about Jake, nor had she heard back from him with a price.

"You know how I told you about my former classmates not being so nice to me?"

Evelyn nodded with a puzzled frown.

"Jake was one of those. And it was ten times worse with him because he was also the dreamiest boy in school in my youthful eyes."

"Well, he's still dreamy, so I can just imagine what young Rachel might have thought," Evelyn answered with a smile before her face flooded with sympathy. "I'm so sorry, Rachel! If I had known I never would have mentioned it to him. I will get right on getting you those other names."

Rachel stepped close and hugged her neighbor. "Don't feel badly. How could you possibly know? And as I said, it wasn't like they really tortured me. It only felt like torture to my underdeveloped teenage brain."

"Doesn't matter. He is now dead to me."

Rachel laughed and actually felt as though she could consider using Jake after all.

"I don't suppose we would mind watching him work in our front yard for a time, would we?"

Evelyn laughed too but still appeared worried.

"Jake promised to get me a price for doing the pier. I haven't heard from him yet, so I haven't made a decision. I would appreciate those other names and numbers but it might not kill me to hire Jake. Or I might wait on the work altogether, since you said you won't hate me forever if I don't do it this year."

"I'll never hate you, I promise," Evelyn declared solemnly making them both laugh again. Sobering, Evelyn clapped her hands together. "Ok, let's get started. Your doors look exactly right and ready for painting. You did an amazing job with removing the existing finish and sanding them smooth. I think they'll turn out really well as long as you buy the right products."

Rachel frowned. "I think I did."

"I'm sure you did. In fact, given how attentive to details you obviously are, it's probably possible you bought even better than necessary." Evelyn glanced down at her clean clothes. "I'd better not jump right in dressed like this. Do you mind if I run home and change first?"

Rachel laughed lightly. "Evelyn, you haven't committed your soul to my little projects. Of course, you can run home and change." She then glanced at a clock. "But do you think maybe you ought to wait until tomorrow to get started with me? If Eric expects you to be resting all day, he might not appreciate coming home to find you up to your elbows in my paint."

Evelyn's face dropped and Rachel wished she could take back her words but didn't do so. She had no intention of being a source of trouble in her friend's marriage.

"I suppose you're right. I just got so excited at the prospect of working on this gorgeous house."

"This gorgeous house will still be here tomorrow. And now that I have the promise of help, I'm going to put aside my work on it until then too and will go get some work done on something else."

"What else are you working on?"

"A work work project," Rachel told her evasively. "I'll tell you about it tomorrow. I think I've had as much confession as I can handle for one day."

Impulsively, Evelyn threw her arms around Rachel and hugged her. After a brief hesitation, Rachel returned the embrace.

Chapter Fourteen

Evelyn was flooded with the first real sense of wellbeing she'd experienced in longer than she ought to have been able to count. It was such a relief to have a new friend. She hadn't even realized how desperately she had missed Eileen until that moment. She would try not to superimpose Rachel over Eileen's memory, that wouldn't help either of them, but Rachel was enough like her aunt to fill the gaping hole that had been left in Evelyn's life.

Eileen had just seemed to get everything. Evelyn didn't think Rachel quite had the same ability, but she seemed to be quite perceptive and had the same warm kind heartedness that her aunt had always exuded.

In that moment, Evelyn didn't even care overly much if she was using her new neighbor as a crutch. If you were broken, a crutch was a necessary tool to healing. And she was most definitely broken. She sighed as she stepped out of the hug she had impetuously thrown at her friend. She probably shouldn't have done it. It was fairly evident that the prickly woman wasn't really the hugging type. But Evelyn most definitely was, and that was the point at that very moment.

But now embarrassed regret was nearly strangling her.

"Well, that was nice," Rachel said in a laugh-filled voice. "I didn't know I needed a hug, too. Now you'd best get out of here before I force a paint brush into your hand."

Evelyn deeply appreciated Rachel's ability to deescalate an awkward situation. She supposed she had a great deal of experience given her stories from high school. Not that it sounded as though she had been terribly successful back then.

Poor little thing. Evelyn's motherly heart went out to the little girl Rachel had been. She tried not to be an extremist, but a part of her wanted to march to the jobsite she knew Jake Callaghan was working on and demand he apologize to Rachel profusely and instantly. But even in her extreme emotions, Evelyn was well aware that Rachel wouldn't thank her for her interference. The fact that Rachel had told Evelyn her experience as though she were disclosing state secrets told Evelyn that she didn't intend to let Jake know how he had scarred her.

But it made Evelyn wonder what else the woman was keeping to herself. She told herself to put a pin in it. She had her own life to overanalyze. She didn't need to do it to Rachel's, too. But examining Rachel's life and trying to solve her problems would help Evelyn avoid the worry that threatened to consume her about her own challenges.

With a sigh, Evelyn waved goodbye and crossed the yard to her own beautiful home. It was true, her house was beautiful. Almost as though a home and garden magazine had thrown up all over it. In the best way possible, of course, she thought with a roll of her eyes. She had thrown all her nesting energy into that house thinking it would be the place they would bring their babies to. But what if there weren't going to be any babies? Despite it being smaller than Rachel's house, it felt to Evelyn as though it echoed with emptiness. She tried to keep music playing always in the background so the lack of childish noises didn't deafen her in the silence. And she had over filled it with stuff. Stupid stuff they would probably have to get rid of if or when they did finally get a child to come live with them.

At this point, Evelyn was willing to consider any option. She had even spent time on the internet trying to discover where the dark web might be. She wasn't sure how people accessed it. She certainly hadn't been able to find it. But she had hoped to find a source for children. She didn't care about its background. She knew full well that she and Eric would be able to provide a wonderful life full of love and opportunities to any child they might be blessed with. But her husband continued to resist the idea of a child not born to them. Evelyn was reasonably sure she would be able to get him to consider adoption, but he was too much of a straight shooter to consider the darker sources she was willing to entertain.

Evelyn didn't care where the child came from; she just wanted children. As many as possible but at least one or two. She probably ought to be in therapy. If Eric was right and it was her head causing her body to reject the babies, she needed to get that straight before they tried again. She even had the name and number of the therapist their fertility doctor recommended. But Evelyn was afraid of what all might come out if she were to delve into the deeper recesses of her own psyche.

Standing at the window, Evelyn allowed herself a few minutes to stare over at Eileen's house. She corrected herself silently. It was Rachel's house now. Maybe she would talk it over with Rachel when she went to help her the next day. Rachel had opened up to her, maybe she ought to do the same. Just thinking about it made her run to the powder room to empty herself of the coffee and muffin she had just enjoyed.

Maybe she would think of something else to talk about the next day.

Chapter Fifteen

Rachel had enjoyed herself far more than she would have expected. Look at her – making friends and getting her life together. It was wonderful.

She wondered when the other shoe was going to drop.

Things never stayed good for Rachel. She didn't expect them to start doing so now after all these years. It nagged at the back of her mind like a little fly that buzzed just out of reach. Enough to be irritating but not sure what to do about it.

Angela and Tina wanted to have another girls' night. Rachel had received the message in the group chat they had set up. It would be fun. Something more to look forward to. But this time it would be at Tina's house. The very prickly Tina who was evidently needing to work very hard at being friendly with her. It actually made Rachel smile to think about.

She had thought she was the prickly one. And she was reasonably certain Evelyn would agree with that assessment. Rachel thought about Evelyn's impulsive hug. It had been nice once she'd gotten over the shock of it. But she felt badly that she had hesitated to return the other woman's gesture. What kind of woman was she that she didn't want new friends hugging her? The prickly sort, that was what. So, she couldn't judge Tina for being the same.

Rachel slept like a log and awoke to a bright new day filled with optimism. She grabbed her laptop and quickly reached her word count goal which she had recently raised to a thousand from the original five hundred. It was already getting easy to do in a short sitting. She often was able to repeat it two or three times throughout the day. Her new story was nearing the halfway point, and she was trying not to be giddy with her delight.

Finally, for the first time in longer than it ought to be, Rachel felt optimism bubbling under the surface of her psyche. It was a beautiful feeling. Rather than the negative feelings that were so often there, now Rachel looked at things with positivity. Maybe this writing thing would work out. Maybe she could make a life for herself and be content, maybe even happy here on Cape Avalon. Maybe she could make and keep friends and surround herself with a network who cared about and supported her.

It was almost a giddy feeling. She didn't know if she ought to trust it, but it buoyed her anyway.

Everything was brighter with this optimism in place. The sky appeared brighter and even her usual toast with peanut butter somehow tasted better than usual. Definitely her coffee was richer and more satisfying. Rachel laughed for no reason other than the joy of being alive. Her own good mood was starting to freak her out. She didn't know how to be Happy Rachel.

She needn't have worried about adjusting. The delight was obviously transient. As soon as she checked her email it shriveled up and floated away on the next stiff breeze coming in off the ocean.

Dear Ms. Whitney:

Thank you for sharing your manuscript with us. We are going to have to pass on it at this time as it does not fit with the direction we are currently taking our catalogue. We wish you all the best in your journey to publication.

Sincerely,

Pauline Chorniak

Rachel refused to cry over something so relatively inconsequential considering the big losses she had suffered that year, but it was a challenge to keep her distress at bay. Her heart sank down to her toes, and she felt worse than she had in weeks.

This was why you shouldn't be happy, she thought fiercely. It made the sadness that much harder to bear. She thought about texting Evelyn to tell her not to come over that day, but she understood how much the other woman was looking forward to helping her. Since she herself had just faced a burdensome disappointment, she couldn't do that to her neighbor even if it was for a far less important reason. Evelyn didn't need to help her paint cupboards in order to keep food on her table. Rachel did need to find a career she could tolerate if she planned to make a life for herself.

Of course, she could sell the cottage and live quite well for years off the proceeds, she was sure. Maybe even the rest of her life if she were to move somewhere with a low cost of living like Mexico or Indonesia. She could still have the beach but not have to worry about supporting herself.

But then what would she actually do?

Finding a career wasn't just about keeping a roof over her head and food on the table. She needed something more meaningful to do with her life than just walking the beach. This is why people had children. But she didn't have any. She only had herself. And she needed to find something to do with this life she had. It might not be the one she had wished for as a child, but it was better than the alternative. And she needed to make the most of it.

But it probably wasn't going to be with a career as an author.

Rachel tried to dredge up some of the optimism she had been feeling by telling herself it was only one agent. If she continued to submit her manuscripts, there would be other opportunities, other requests, perhaps an acceptance or two. She shouldn't give up yet. But in that moment, she just wanted to curl up and go back to bed. Pulling the covers back over her head and sleeping this day away was sounding more appealing by the moment.

Her next email was from Jake. He finally had her quote. Even with the former classmate discount he was touting, it was an eye-opening amount. Not as huge as she had feared, but she had hoped her highest guess was way, way higher than it could possibly be. Most of her wanted to just deleted his email and continue with her new plan of sleeping until she had to go back to Chicago and take back her forensic accountant position.

Instead, she girded herself mentally and replied to Jake's email.

Jake,

Thanks for the quote.

Is there a possibility of a less expensive way of rebuilding? Like with wood instead of this special concrete?

Rachel

She didn't need proper salutations. They weren't friends.

Despite everything, she felt badly about the abrupt email after she hit send. With a silent groan, Rachel started up the breathing exercises she had been taught to try to alleviate some of the stress spike she was experiencing. It wouldn't do to give herself a heart attack or an aneurism or some such medical horror.

The breathing did help, but Rachel knew she needed something even more powerful. A walk on the beach would help her get her panicky sensations under control. And she didn't think Evelyn was due very soon. She could surely go and be back before Evelyn came knocking.

By the time Rachel returned to her house, the ocean breezes, cold but gentle that day, had blown out the worst of her dark feelings. She was far from the optimistic creature she had woken up as, but that creature was a foreigner in Rachel's body and she didn't need to be overly concerned about its absence. If she was at her usual level of resigned sadness, Rachel could live with that.

But the disappointment did color her day in darker shades. Even Evelyn noticed.

"You are quieter than usual today. Did you sleep poorly?"

Rachel tried to smile at her friendly neighbor, but she knew it was half-hearted at best. "My sleep was fine. I just got a few stressful emails first thing this morning."

"Is that why you were pounding the sand so early?" Evelyn asked with a light laugh. "That's an excellent way to manage stress."

"It is, I agree. Which is part of why I am really hoping that I can make a go of staying here."

"What will determine it? Can I help somehow?"

Rachel laughed. "Would you rather I sell so some sweet family could move in here instead?" She realized her error as soon as it left her mouth but she couldn't retract the words, instead tried to lighten it with more. "You must be so popular on this lane with all your baking. I'm surprised I haven't seen more children lined up around your house like the pied piper."

Evelyn's pleasant face didn't fall but she shook her head. "I don't bake for the neighborhood children. For one thing, so many of the moms have their kids on gluten free or some other restrictions so I wouldn't want to overstep that."

Rachel knew she had put her foot in it and wished she could rewind the morning. She didn't think she was such a miserable person that she wanted others to feel badly with her. She just hadn't thought through her words before they came out of her mouth.

"Anyway, no I would rather stick with the neighbor I'm getting to know if I get any say in the matter," she added with another light laugh. "Besides, neither of us are too very old just yet. It's still possible that both of us might still populate the lane."

While Rachel wanted to recoil from the suggestion, she didn't want to hurt her friend any more than she already had, so she just smiled even if it wasn't very sincere.

When Rachel didn't say anything, Evelyn prompted her. "So, what would it take? You didn't say."

Rachel sighed. "I need to be able to make money. I only have enough saved up for my temporary sabbatical. I need a permanent or at least semi-permanent way of having an income."

"So, what are your options? I'm assuming you would prefer remote work so you can stay here rather than having a commute? Or would you consider driving in to the city? It only takes Eric about an hour most days unless there's truly awful weather."

"No, you're right, I would prefer to avoid the commute. If I could get work in the village, that might be nice, to get me out and exposed to people despite my inclination to be a hermit. But it would be truly ideal to be able to work from home on my own time and schedule."

"Could you or would you even want to do your accounting work from here? Would your old boss go for that, do you think?"

"It's possible. I didn't float that idea to them yet. But as I mentioned before, I'm a little burned out from that work after the experiences I've had."

"So, what else have you looked into?"

They had continued to paint the doors throughout this conversation but Rachel put down her roller in order to be able to properly answer the intense question.

Well, it wasn't intense on Evelyn's part. But Rachel's reaction to it required a break from the paint.

"I've written a novel and I've been submitting it to agents." Rachel said the words as though she were confessing her greatest sins.

Evelyn stared at her with a suitably shocked expression on her face before her mouth split into a wide grin and she was laughing and clapping her hands despite the paintbrush in them.

"That is so exciting, Rachel! I can't believe it. Or rather I can, since I knew you were so smart. And your aunt loved reading so much, so I suppose she passed that onto you. Did she know?"

The last question was on a lower octave, almost as though Evelyn was afraid to ask.

"She knew and loved hearing about my stories. I wish she were still here to know that I finally finished one."

"Oh, have you written many?"

"I would say I have dozens started."

"Dozens? Oh my! I can't even imagine!" Evelyn's admiring gaze did a little to bolster Rachel's lagging confidence. It was true that most people never got around to writing the novel they all say they want to do.

"Only one is fully completed. It's probably a mess but there's a beginning, a middle, and an end. Up until recently, I could never write the end. I think it was some sort of psychological quagmire."

"Quagmire. Is that the type of books you're writing? With words like quagmire in them? They might not gain as much commercial success."

Rachel laughed. "Well, they are historicals, so I think you can get away with a certain level of vocabulary there. But no, I try not to let my love of words go too crazy in my stories. That was one thing Aunt Eileen was always on about. That I needed to be true to my time period but still be readable for today."

"This is so exciting! I never knew a real person who has written a book. I'm so thrilled for you."

"Yeah, but I got a rejection this morning."

"Ah, I see. Is that why you were beating up the sand with your feet this morning?"

Rachel laughed at her turn of phrase but shrugged and nodded sheepishly. "It stung since I had gotten my hopes up. I should have known better than to do that. But I couldn't help it."

"Well, that was just one agent, there are surely plenty more out there who will love to represent your book." She paused for second, wrinkling her nose. "Have you considered self-publishing or are you one of those literary types who considers it beneath you?"

Rachel laughed again, feeling relief from having shared her burden. "Well," she began hesitantly. "I'm not sure you could call me a literary type, and I certainly don't think it's beneath me. I actually think my accountant brain might appreciate the business side of publishing myself. But how will I know if it's any good? That's the thing with going the traditional route, if the big companies take you, you can be confident it's good."

"I don't mean to be a downer, but I've read plenty of books that weren't so great. Or maybe I should say they weren't to my taste. I don't think that is the way to judge if it's good. I think the fact that they get taken up by an agent or a big company is because they think it's commercially viable, but that doesn't mean it's good or not."

Rachel huffed a sigh, not sure what to make of her friend's words. "How do you seem to be informed on this topic? Have you been writing?"

Evelyn laughed. "I wish. No, I'm not that smart. Or I can't hold all the necessary threads together in my head, anyway. My sister in Boston is friends with a writer who seems to be really successful. I'm on her Advanced Reader Review team so I get a little bit of the inside scoop from her. She was published with one of those New York companies for a while, but she decided to go independent when she saw how small the fraction of money was actually making its way into her bank account."

"Hmm. That's interesting. But at least she already had the validation of having been traditionally published."

Evelyn shrugged. "I think she was more concerned about her wallet. And it sounds to me like that's a concern for you, too, isn't it? So that you can stay here?"

Rachel bit her lip and nodded. "But I only have five months to decide. And trying to start publishing my books might make that time shorter if I have to spend very much for editors and covers and whatever else I don't even know about yet. And it still might not sell if it's no good."

"Do you want me to ask this writer that I read for if she would consider reading your book and give you a little advice? She seems very nice. I don't think she would mind at all."

"Oh, I don't know," Rachel hesitated, her insides warring between embarrassment and ambition. "Don't you think that would seem presumptuous?"

Evelyn frowned in thought. "Maybe if you reached out directly, although I really don't think she's the type to think like that. But especially if I ask her, the worst that can happen is she says no. Even if she was furious, which would be ridiculous, the very worst that would happen is she'd kick me off her ARC team. That would be so rude that I might not buy her books but I still could if I wanted to."

Rachel laughed a little over her friend's words but they also really touched her. She no longer felt completely in the depths of despair even if she was undecided about asking a stranger for advice. Confiding in Evelyn had been even more helpful to her mindset than she had anticipated.

"I'm going to ask her. I won't name names so she doesn't even have to know it's you in case you've run across her or maybe you will in the future. I'll just straight up ask her if she would consider anything like that. I'll message her privately, not in the ARC team group, that way she won't be inundated with people wanting the same thing. All she can do is say yes or no."

"Oh Evelyn, thank you so much. I love your persistence even when I'm mired in uncertainty."

"Well, it's understandable that your confidence is a little shaken after getting a rejection, I suppose. Decisions are hard when that happens. Believe me, I know."

With a wobbly smile exchanged the pair got back to their painting. Before Rachel realized, they had the first coat done on all the doors and cupboards.

"Evelyn!" she exclaimed. "I never would have believed it. I thought this would take days for each coat."

"It's not that much square footage," Evelyn pointed out reasonably, making Rachel laugh.

"Maybe not, but I am very new to the DIY scene for one thing. For another, I wasn't sure if the fumes would be too overwhelming for us to be able to stick with the job."

"You bought the right products," Evelyn nodded with approval. "Also, every job is less than half when you have help."

"How true," Rachel agreed with a giggle. "But we did work through lunch."

"And you don't have the spare tire to lose like I have," Evelyn gestured to her tummy. "You ought to eat something."

"We both ought to," Rachel insisted. "Just something light or we won't eat supper. How about I whip us up a wrap?"

Evelyn nodded even though she appeared uncertain over what exactly Rachel was offering her, making Rachel laugh again. Even though she still felt a little despairing about the possibility of being able to support herself with her writing, she was much more settled mentally than she had been first thing that morning.

"How are the rest of your renovations coming along?" Evelyn evidently didn't love silence as much as Rachel did and filled the space with conversation. Rachel didn't mind, though. She could probably make the simple chicken salad wraps in her sleep.

"I'm not doing anything other than replacing some fixtures, repairing some cracks, and repainting so it's more of a crack fill than a renovation."

"Still, it's a lot of work to take on yourself."

Rachel shrugged. "It hasn't been too bad," she said with a smile, surprised at the level of pride she felt in that statement. "I'm pretty much done upstairs. Except my aunt's room. I can't make myself go in there yet." She didn't want to talk about it so she hurried to add, "And now, with your help, this floor is nearly finished."

"Are you going to replace any of the flooring?"

"Possibly in the bathroom down here. For some reason it seems to have had the most wear and tear. If I can't get the grout cleaned to my satisfaction, I'll have to replace all the tiles."

"That will be a big job," Evelyn commiserated. "You should try baking soda."

Rachel laughed, leaning over to put her arm around Evelyn in a side hug. It had been far too long that she had comfortable female company. Really any comfortable company, but she was finding more and more that female company was a psychological need she had not been filling for far too long. Even with Aunt Eileen, the visits had been too infrequent to be considered a part of her daily life aside from phone calls and messages. Still there was a gaping wound in her life where Aunt Eileen had once been. But Rachel was seeing that developing some friendships just might help her survive.

"Maybe I ought to see about getting some freelance accounting work."

"Oh no, don't give up on your dreams just yet," Evelyn cried out as though she were getting too invested in Rachel's plans. The thought made Rachel smile until she realized that the poor woman probably had too many shaky dreams of her own, she wanted to see someone's succeed.

"I'm not giving up, just maybe buying myself a little more time. My thinking was very all or nothing, I think. If I can get a bit of freelance work with the accompanying pay, it will give me longer to stay here and decide what I'm doing. If there's even a slight possibility that I might try doing indie publishing, I will need a bit bigger nest egg than I have. Besides, Jake's quote was enough to curl my hair."

Evelyn laughed. "And you being an accountant, you can't just go with the flow on the financial side."

Rachel lifted a shoulder and knew her smile was lopsided but she did her best. "I tried that. It didn't work out so well for me," she added. "I ought to be in a position of never needing to work again."

Evelyn stared. "Would you like that? Wouldn't that be boring?"

Rachel laughed a little. "Maybe. But wouldn't it be nice to have the choice? Right now, I have few choices."

"Very well, then, I vote for you finding a freelance job if it means you can stay here longer and maybe forever and also not giving up on the dream."

Feeling cheered, Rachel's laughter was more genuine this time. "Thanks for the vote."

"Do you know where you'll find this kind of work?"

"Yeah," she said slowly. "My problem will be keeping it in bounds. I suspect there will be tons of work out there I could take on. But I still want this time to heal. I want to have as much free time as I need to daydream and walk on the beach and just restore myself, you know?"

"Oh, I definitely know."

"What about you, Evie? How are your dreams coming along?"

Evelyn held her breath as though trying to hold in her secrets. "I've been researching adoption and fostering," she blurted out in a rush as though she couldn't hold it in anymore.

"That's wonderful, Ev! How does Eric feel about it?"

"I haven't told him yet."

There was a beat of silence while both women absorbed that information, and then Rachel pulled her friend in for a quick hug.

"Should there be wine with our wraps?" Rachel asked even as she was pulling a bottle out of her fridge. "Half a glass at least. Surely, we deserve it after the morning we've had. Besides, didn't that country singer say it's five o'clock somewhere?"

Evelyn's chuckle sounded a little forced, but Rachel didn't look at her to verify. She only hoped the woman wasn't crying. Rachel was happy to have a new friend, but her own psychological state was a little too shaky to be able to take on the other woman's emotions. And these ones were big. Rachel wasn't overly aware of her own maternal urges, but she knew they were powerful once they activated. And Evelyn seemed to have them in bucket loads. Rachel knew she ought to do more than just offer lunch to the woman, but she didn't have much to draw from.

Within minutes they were back out on the porch with blankets thrown over their laps to ward off the November chill.

"Has there ever been a snowfall since you've lived on the island, Evelyn?"

"No, have you ever seen one?" Evelyn sounded a mixture of shock and delight making Rachel giggle.

"I haven't seen one either, but Eileen said it has happened. She lived here year-round for nearly all her adult life. I'm really hoping this isn't the year for it to recur, though, I'm sorry if that will disappoint you.

After spending nearly a decade in Chicago, with the heavy winters we got there, I'm thrilled to be just in a sweater now, even at the end of November."

"You'll acclimatize and find this to be extra cold, don't worry."

"Oh, no, I'm so sorry, I didn't think of that. Are you freezing?"

Evelyn laughed. "Nope. This blanket is doing its job quite nicely, thank you."

They settled into comfortable silence for a few minutes while they munched their snack. Finally, Rachel broke the silence.

"Did you find that it will be difficult or easy to go the adoption or fostering route? Or is it still too touchy to discuss?"

"No, I want to talk about it, I think. My heart just wants kiddos to love, you know? I don't really feel that they need to be of my body although that would be nice, too. It would have been ideal if we could have just popped out some little ones that were a part of each of us. But that doesn't seem to be working for us. And I would rather fill my house than not just because of the biological connection." Evelyn sighed making Rachel wonder if perhaps her husband didn't agree with her, but she wasn't ready to delve into that topic with her new friend.

"As to whether or not it will be easy or hard. I think challenging might be the right word. Which it ought to be really. They shouldn't just hand out children to anyone who asks, of course. And I know we will qualify. But there are many hoops to jump through, so much paperwork, and some of it feels pretty invasive. I haven't started the process yet. I do need Eric to agree. And I don't think he's going to like someone poking around in our lives to the extent that they'll have to. But I like to know exactly what I'm dealing with, you know? If this next round doesn't take, I want to feel like there are still options. And even if it does take, I don't want to have only one child. I think he or she would be lonely."

She paused and looked at Rachel with apologies written all over her face, making Rachel laugh right out loud.

"Don't even worry about it, Evelyn. If I had a child, I wouldn't really want him or her to be the only one either. Not that I feel that was what blighted my life. There were advantages to being an only. But especially if you plan to raise them here, in a smaller community where there are fewer children, I would agree completely that siblings would be great."

Evelyn's smile was still tentative, but Rachel didn't bother arguing further. The poor woman would have to find her own path to confidence. Rachel certainly wasn't in a position to give her directions.

"Anyhow. I'm glad to have some contact information and some places to start. When I'm ready, I'll talk to Eric about it and we'll see where we can go from there. I'm sure he'll want to wait and see if we can get pregnant and carry this baby to term."

The way she trailed off made Rachel think there was more to it.

"But you'd like to get on the waiting list, is that right?"

"Yes, exactly."

"Did you get any idea how long that could take? If it's years, then I'd agree with you. If it's weeks or months, then you'd probably be good to hold off until you see how your treatment goes. I know I wouldn't want to be experiencing a high-risk pregnancy and then have a troubled child brought into my home."

Evelyn bit her lip. "No, I guess I can see what you mean. But the foster or adopted children don't necessarily have to be troubled," she protested.

"Perhaps not every single one, but I would say most probably are to at least a certain extent. Unless you get an infant, they will be struggling with separation at the very least. And an infant would probably be dealing with some sort of withdrawal."

Evelyn's eyes filled with tears. "Do you think it's a stupid idea?"

"Not in the least," Rachel declared immediately. "Any child would be lucky to have you take it into your life. Especially a troubled one. I think you have a heart big enough to handle whatever might come your way. I just don't think during your pregnancy would be the healthiest time to take it on."

"But what about when our natural child is little? Am I foolish to even consider it?"

"I don't think so," Rachel said with a tinge of hesitation. "There are risks to anything, especially anything that involves opening your heart and your home. I'm sure if you foster or adopt there will be supports put in place to help you, especially at first." She hesitated again before continuing. "This is something you and your husband will have to think about really hard both together and independently as you both have to be firmly on board for it to work, but I think it's an amazing thing that you're even considering it. I don't know where I would have ended up if Aunt Eileen hadn't opened her heart and her home to me, and at such an awkward age. Imagine taking a grieving thirteen-year-old into your home?"

Evelyn grinned. "I'm sure you were delightful."

"I wasn't, I can promise you that. But Aunt Eileen's heart was wide enough. And I know yours is, too."

"Aww, that's the sweetest thing anyone has ever said to me." Evelyn sniffled a little, worrying Rachel. Rachel didn't yet feel emotionally strong herself to be able to manage her friend's deep emotions. To her relief, Evelyn rallied.

"You're right, I have to talk to Eric about this. But you're also right that I need to think about it on my own for a bit, too. I feel like I really want to do this, but I'm not sure if it's just my mothering urge talking and stirring up my emotions."

"Emotions aren't bad," Rachel reminded her, even though she herself sometimes considered them so. But it earned her a beaming smile from Evelyn.

"Do you think it's ready for a second coat?" Evelyn asked eagerly, making Rachel stare at her.

"I thought you were the experienced one," she said.

"What do you mean?"

"The can said you need at least 4 to 6 hours between coats depending on the humidity. I would think right next to the shore like this we might need even more. I don't plan to touch that stuff again until tomorrow at the earliest."

Evelyn looked around in dismay after Rachel had gathered up their plates and glasses. "But how will you live like this?"

Rachel laughed. "It'll be fine. It will only be a few days. A week at the most, probably, before I can put everything away. I should still be able to cook, but if it gets too annoying, there's always takeout."

"Oh no, you ought to come stay with us. It'll be better for you to get out of the fumes, and then we can make sure you're fed."

Rachel was divided. It was a generous offer, but she didn't want to accept it. "That is so sweet of you Evelyn, but I am still in a state of needing my own space, with grieving and trying to figure out my life. I'm sure you understand since you have big decisions to make, too."

To Rachel's relief, Evelyn didn't seem hurt or put out by her words. She nodded sagely. "I see what you mean. But do knock whenever you want a meal."

Rachel grinned and nodded, not committing to anything.

"And I'll be back tomorrow for that next coat," Evelyn promised as she headed out the door. Rachel waved and shut the door behind her neighbor, sinking to the floor against the door.

Evelyn was right, her house was a disaster. But it was a controlled disaster, Rachel assured herself. It was on the road to repair. Once the cupboards were done and any more painting she was going to do on that floor, it was only the bathroom tiles that would be left. Maybe she should try Evelyn's baking soda trick right now.

She stayed right where she was on the floor. There was really no rush. And she was much too tired. Her feelings had been on too much of a rollercoaster ride in the past few days. With restoring old friendships, making a new one, and experiencing the most optimistic feelings she had in ages, maybe ever, the ride had been mostly positive. But today had been very bumpy. It probably wasn't healthy to be so volatile emotionally. It was probably just part of the grieving process, she assured herself, but it wasn't any fun, that was for sure.

Getting up from the floor, Rachel dusted off her bottom and decided to turn her back on the mess for a bit. She then grabbed her laptop and retreated to the front room where she had designated her office.

The house was big enough that there was plenty of room for her to claim more than one for herself.

Chapter Sixteen

Rachel sat down at her desk that faced out overlooking the beach. From the vantage point of the second floor, she could see pretty far. It was a lovely clear day and the beach invited her, but she knew it was cold and blustery despite the appearances otherwise.

And she had things to do.

Freelance work. Was she ready to dip her toes back into accounting? It hadn't even been two months since she had been shattered by the double devastation of her husband's death and then finding out all the secrets he had kept from her.

The financial devastation hadn't been nearly as hard to take as finding out he wasn't the man she had thought him to be. Even though they hadn't felt as warm and fuzzy toward each other as they had when they were young, Rachel had thought they were still friends. She had told Todd everything. He knew all about her attempts at writing, even though he had belittled them. He knew she didn't have any friends. He knew she missed her aunt. He knew she loved her job. He knew all her coworkers. Everything. And she had thought she knew everything about him. Of course, she wasn't completely stupid. It had been obvious he didn't share as many details with her as she did with him, but she had always chalked that up to him being a guy and not feeling the need to share as much as a woman needed to. But no. It had turned out that he had too many secrets that he didn't want her to find out about.

Maybe going back into accounting wasn't the best idea after all. Rachel sighed. What else could she do, though? She didn't really have any other skills.

Don't sell yourself so short. Her mindset group would be appalled with how far down she had allowed herself to get today. Blowing a stray hair off her forehead, Rachel opened a search engine and started investigating. That was one aspect of forensic accounting she could still do – research and investigation. She would figure out what sort of work there might be for her.

A couple hours later she came back up for air. The room had darkened as the sun was setting, and her stomach was reminding her that she ought to eat something. But she was also reminded that having a flexible schedule would be perfect. Being able to chase down ideas whenever she felt like it would be amazing. And being able to go out for a walk or a swim whenever she felt like it and the weather permitted was a luxury she didn't want to give up too soon.

There were a few possibilities for work she could do. But she knew her best bet for getting work she would enjoy and that would easily pay her few bills lay in the accounting sphere. If she had even just one client, she wouldn't have to worry about money. Since her house was paid for, she only had to really pay utilities, taxes, and food. She could live as simply or as lavishly as she could afford. If she could get a little paid work that would keep her fed, she could use her savings to finish the house repairs and support her pursuit for publication. If she could find someone to reassure her that her work was acceptable.

That was the biggest problem. Her confidence had been shattered. Finding out your husband was living a lie when you were supposed to be a detail-oriented person would do that to a woman, apparently, Rachel thought sarcastically as she made her way back down to the kitchen.

Her thoughts had made her appetite flee, but she would make herself a healthy snack anyway. Grief was not a weight loss method she would recommend to anyone, but for her it was certainly effective. But she needed to be careful. Even though most women appreciated a slender frame, she didn't want to overdo it and start looking like a skeleton. Aunt Eileen wouldn't want that. And Rachel knew she was grieving more for her aunt than for Todd. Or perhaps she was mourning the loss of the boy she had once known. The one she had married originally. Because the man she had been living with for the last several years had most definitely no longer been him.

Despite the darkness that had fallen and the bite to the air, Rachel knew she needed the restorative experience of a walk on the beach. She wouldn't go far as she was a big chicken, but she couldn't stay in the house with her thoughts.

She had ended up going further than she had planned, so it was nearly full on dark by the time she returned to her own beachfront. Rachel was grateful for the brightness of the moon reflecting off the sand as all the plants and dunes that were so beautiful in the sunlight had started to take on mysterious shapes that, with her active imagination, were giving her a strong case of the shivers.

That could be the cold, too, she thought with a slight chuckle, grateful that her walk had lifted her mood considerably.

But the sound of her laugh brought another shape into movement. Someone was on her beach. A man from the shape of him. Fear lodged itself firmly in her chest. She shouldn't have come out by herself. She ought to get a dog. She ought to have a weapon, even a walking stick, for occasions such as this. She was terrifying herself, and it might be needlessly.

Rachel eyed the distance to her front porch, calculating how fast she could get there.

"Rachel, is that you?"

"Jake?" Fear morphed into fury. "What are you doing out here skulking in the dark?"

"I wasn't skulking," he replied with a laugh, not seemingly offended. "I just didn't calculate the sun setting on me."

"You didn't answer my question," Rachel retorted, not willing to be swayed by the dimple that peeped out of his cheek when he had laughed. She was finally close enough that she could see him properly in the moonlight. She shouldn't have gotten that close. Despite the fact that he looked like he had been working all day, he smelled quite delicious, like he had stepped out of the shower and the pine-scented soap still clung to him. But that was a ridiculous thought that Rachel refused to entertain. Neither would she stare at how well his long-sleeved t-shirt and faded jeans clung to his evidently well-worked body.

She might be skinny from her grief, but she was far from fit. She was a little jealous of the shape the man was in. And he shouldn't be skulking on her property in the dark.

Jake sighed. "My apologies, Rach, I should have called or texted or something. This is the second time I've startled you, isn't it? You're not going to want to hire me even if you ought to." He shook his head and took a step away from her. "I wanted to get another look at your waterfront. Since you asked about other, cheaper ways to build your pier and protect your property, I needed to take another look, as I only had the concrete type in mind when I was here before. And I felt like a walk anyway, so I parked at my friend's house down a ways and walked over. I didn't think I'd run into you, so I didn't bother telling you I was coming. I really am sorry. I realize in hindsight that you don't really know me anymore, so you could find me frightening if you came across me unannounced."

"Which I have now done twice," she pointed out crisply. "And I never knew you, so yes, a large man lurking in the dark is a scary thing."

"What do you mean, you never knew me?" Jake's shock sounded genuine.

Rachel felt her chin drop open in surprise. But she quickly shut it and shook her head. She didn't have it in her to get into this with him. He wasn't her friend. She was doing her best to keep herself sane. She didn't need a Jake visitation to derail the progress she had just made on her walk.

"Never mind that, Jake, did you come to any conclusions while you were looking at my property?"

"I did. I think you're right. Since your neighbors on both sides have the full concrete retention-type piers, you could probably get away with wood. But while that would be cheaper in the short term, it will need replacing again much sooner down the road than concrete would need."

Rachel nodded. That made sense. It was something she would have to think about. Since she still didn't know what she was going to do with her life and with this house, it was hard to decide.

"You don't have to do this project right away, though. Especially not in the winter. While we do work year-round, working in the water in the winter doesn't hold a great deal of appeal."

Rachel was sure he was trying to be charming, but she tried not to let it affect her. The dimple carving a hole in his cheek when he grinned didn't help her much with that endeavor, though, so she averted her gaze.

Her heart wasn't slowing down as quickly from the fright as she would have expected. It disgusted her to think she might find Jake attractive. While she was trying to be reasonable and stop holding a grudge against Jake for the life she ended up with, he was still a part of the torment she faced in high school. From reports she read in the news, the teasing she had faced as a kid was nothing like the bullying many children endured today with the advent of technology and such, but still, it had felt like torment to the sensitive teenager she had been, and she wasn't ready to forgive him for that.

Jake kicked the sand. "So, how are you settling in here? Is it uncomfortable for you being back in your aunt's house without her?" He paused and despite the darkness, Rachel knew he was blushing, and again she fought against a twinge of attraction. "Of course, it's uncomfortable; it would be sad, at the very least. I should have rather asked, is it getting better? Or do you think you're going to have to sell?"

Rachel surprised them both with a little puff of laughter. "I wouldn't sell for that reason. Being in her house makes it almost feel like I still have a piece of her, and that will be the part that would be the hardest about selling. And it isn't so bad. I mean, of course I'm grieving, but the house is the comfort not the cause. I'm settling in. I am loving it more here than I ever could have thought possible."

"Didn't you expect to? I mean, you did live here as a youngster." The clueless man seemed puzzled, and Rachel wanted to kick him in the shins.

"I didn't have the very best of experiences when I lived here, and then I moved away and never visited, so I wasn't sure how it would feel."

Jake nodded and shuffled his feet with discomfort.

"Are you going to sell in the spring? It will probably be a really hot market."

"Are you in the market for a house? Is that why you're asking?" Rachel sounded belligerent and didn't even care.

"No," he protested with the sound of almost anger in his tone. "Do you think I'm angling to get you out so I could buy your house? What kind of a jerk do you think I am?"

"Jake, it's late, and I'm more tired than I even realized. I worked hard all day and had a few disappointments along the way. I think I'll take my leave before this escalates," Rachel said, sounding defeated, and took a step as though to turn away, but he reached out and grabbed her arm. It wasn't a strong hold; she could have broken away easily, but the fact that he would touch her froze her to her place. She was both frightened and comforted by his touch in a disturbing maelstrom of confusion.

"Wait, I'm sorry, don't go. Of course, you think I'm a jerk. I was a jerk to you when we were kids. I'm surprised you'll even speak to me, so I shouldn't expect you to think any differently of me now." He dropped his hand and sighed. "I'm actually surprised you would even consider my quote."

"I don't want the house to wash away," she said with an awkward little laugh.

"You could get a company from the mainland to come out here for something like this. There are a few with the special equipment. A bigger company might be able to give you as good a price as I gave you."

Rachel frowned. "Do you not want to do it?"

146

"I do, but I don't want you to be uncomfortable. I'd rather you got someone else, so you don't have to remember any uncomfortable memories or whatever is happening right now."

Rachel laughed. She wasn't sure what was happening right now, but it wasn't uncomfortable memories. "I appreciate the consideration, Jake. But I'll also appreciate your adjusted quotation."

She saw a flash of white where he smiled but she knew he still seemed uneasy with her since he was still shuffling his feet. He'd make a terrible poker player, Rachel realized and wanted to laugh again. She wondered if there had been similar tells when they were kids and she had just been too young to read them. With a soft sigh and a mental shrug, Rachel turned her back on the past for a moment.

"Have you always stayed on the island?" Rachel surprised herself. She hadn't meant to invite further conversation, had she?

Jake seemed almost as surprised as she felt, but it might have been puzzlement over the awkward wording of her question. For a writer, she wasn't being terribly coherent.

"Do you mean, like, did I never move away after school finished?"

Rachel nodded even though he probably couldn't see her very clearly in the dim light.

"I did move away for a while, after graduation. Bummed around for a couple of years, actually."

Rachel was swept with a wave of curiosity. What must that have been like? She had exerted so much structure over her life for years until now, and even now she had various requirements of herself. She couldn't even begin to imagine what "bumming around" might feel like.

"Did you go to school?" she asked before realizing that was the worst question.

"We weren't all as smart as you," he reminded her without rancor. "I did eventually take some trade school to make sure I could work legally and take out the right permits. But not academia like I heard you did."

She nodded again despite the moonlight and persisted in pursuing her curiosity. "What did bumming around look like? Where did you go? What did you see? How did you live? I don't remember your parents being terribly wealthy, so I can't imagine they supported you in a life of luxury."

"Oh, there wasn't much luxurious about it," Jake returned with a dry chuckle. "But it was interesting and an education in and of itself." He paused and turned slightly so he was gazing out to sea. "I mostly just moved around a lot, doing odd jobs to keep myself fed. Stayed in hostels and cheap hotels until I made friends and could couch surf in whatever new place I'd found. That way, I could save up enough to get to the next place."

Rachel couldn't even begin to imagine that experience but was fascinated by it none the less.

"I have barely seen anywhere outside of a classroom or an office," she said in way of response, and even she could hear jealousy in her voice, making them both laugh. "Did you have a favorite place? Where's the most exotic place you went? Did you leave the country?"

Jake laughed again but held up his hand to stem the flow of her questions. "You seem to be fired up with your curiosity and don't look quite as cold as you were a minute ago when you were shivering. I shouldn't keep you standing here talking all night."

Rachel was swept with embarrassment and wished a tsunami would conveniently sweep her out of the awkward moment. "Oh, no, I shouldn't keep you chatting. I'm sure you weren't expecting to be accosted by a curious bystander. I'm so sorry. Goodnight," she babbled the jumble of words and was about to flee when he stopped her again with a hand on her arm.

"I didn't mean that in the least, Rach, but you were shivering. If you were to offer me a coffee sometime, I'd love to tell you all about it."

Rachel blinked and had to concentrate not to let her mouth fall open in surprise. Had she invited him to spend more time with her? The thought should have repulsed her. But it didn't. She was actually curious about his nomadic youth. It would feed her desire to travel. And maybe could set her on the path of a good place to set as her first destination.

She had enjoyed the trips she had taken with Aunt Eileen, but they had often returned to places they enjoyed and hadn't been overly imaginative in their destinations to begin with. Certainly, Jake would have far more knowledge about travel than she had.

But offer him a coffee and plan to sit and chat with him? Was he nuts? She didn't think she'd ever be that evolved emotionally.

"Sure, we'll chat sometime," she managed to choke out, not interested in explaining why that might be stretching the truth. "Have a good night, Jake," she called out as she walked away, hoping he didn't stop her again.

"You too, Rach." It was weird what hearing him shorten her name like that in his deep, chocolatey voice did to her. She hadn't had that sort of a visceral reaction to a guy since she was a teenager. Well, she supposed, since the last time she knew Jake. No one called her Rach, either. Or no one in her Chicago life ever did. She was Rachel. Spelled out. Buttoned up. No nonsense. No fun, as Todd would say. But that was who she was. Or who she had been for a time, at least.

Rachel didn't really know who she was anymore. All her personal identifying markers were gone. She wasn't currently an accountant. She was no one's wife. She had no family. She didn't live in the same place nor know any of the same people she had known for her entire adult life.

She was adrift on a brand new sea with very little navigation equipment.

But for the first time in her life, she felt prepared for the adventure that was about to unfold. Delight filled her and pushed out the negative feelings that had jangled her nerves while speaking with Jake. She had been able to speak with him and not fall apart. And all of it, including the long walk, had reordered her thoughts sufficiently that she expected to sleep quite soundly.

Chapter Seventeen

S he did. Rachel slept like the proverbial log and was almost surprised when the sunlight streaming through the crack between the curtains woke her up. Stretching and yawning, Rachel was surprised to feel much more rested than she could ever remember feeling.

Doing a mental self-assessment, Rachel recognized a few aches from where she had been hunched over painting the day before, but she determined it wasn't anything a few more stretches wouldn't work out. She also realized that she was feeling steady. In her mind, in her heart, she didn't feel in the depths of despair like she had been the day before when she'd read her email.

After sitting up and fluffing the pillows behind her back against the wall, Rachel pulled her laptop toward her and quickly dashed off her first one thousand words for the day. The story was flowing, her fingers were flying, and a sense of well-being permeated her.

Rachel didn't think she would be able to come up with as happy an ending for herself as she was planning for her characters, but she could live vicariously through them, she assured herself as she allowed the plot to thicken in her manuscript but tried to keep the end goal in mind. Despite her own darkness, she was striving for a light tone in her book.

No need to bleed her own lifeblood out onto the pages of what she intended to be escapist entertainment for her readers.

If she ever got readers.

That worry niggled at the back of her mind. She was able to ignore it long enough to bypass her daily word count goal but when she saved and closed her document, Rachel knew she couldn't ignore it much longer. She had spent a bit of time the day before searching for freelance options, but today, in a better frame of mind, she thought she might be more successful. And she also felt more prepared to take on a bit of work. Especially if she kept it to a day or two each week, she'd still be able to write and finish her house projects. And the income would basically give her an infinite amount of time to decide what she was going to do.

It also might be easier to exit from a freelance gig than a "real" job if she ever did find some financial success from her writing. That held definite appeal. She had been flooded with guilt when she had told her old employer that she was leaving. And they still didn't want to accept it, promising her that her position would always be open.

But Rachel knew she was never going back to Chicago. Not to live anyway. She didn't hold a grudge against the city itself, but it hadn't been a very happy place for her. She couldn't see herself settling there even if it didn't work out for her to stay on the Cape. She knew she would need to ensure she was always closer to the ocean in the future whatever might happen.

Maybe she would find somewhere tropical to live, she thought with a grin as she pulled up her email system. Rachel had the idea that one of her old clients might be looking to hire her type of services on a part-time prolonged basis. She would reach out to her old contact. It would be interesting work and definitely good enough pay. She wasn't sure if it would work out since the small company had ended their contract with Rachel's firm nearly a year previously, hiring someone to do their accounting in-house. But Rachel had maintained professional contact with the CEO. Despite Chicago being such a big city, the business world could often be very small. Contacting them wouldn't violate the non-compete contract Rachel had with her firm. She knew they would be happy for her to find her footing, even if that included not returning to work for them after her sabbatical. That certainty was a comfort.

Just as she hit send on the message she had composed, she received the notification of an incoming message from Evelyn.

Rachel! I knew she wouldn't mind. You know that author I mentioned? Catherine Stewart? She'd love to speak with you. Here's her contact information. I'll see you a little later for the next coat. I'm so excited to hear what you think of her...

Rachel stared at her friend's message and felt the usual flock of butterflies take flight in her tummy. She was nervous about reaching out to a stranger at the best of times, let alone when it was something so vulnerable as sharing her writing. But Rachel reminded herself, if she wanted to actually make a go of being a writer and earning an income from that pursuit, she really needed to be willing to share it with others.

Taking a deep breath, Rachel opened a new message and started to type. But she didn't get very far.

Was this a pen name?

Should she be formal or informal?

Would "dear" be too weird? Well, no, you use dear on every correspondence. It's an accepted convention.

With a groan, Rachel swallowed down the impulse to throw her laptop across the room. It wasn't the computer's fault that she was being a dolt. She did her breathing exercises for two minutes to get the panic under control and then she began again.

Hello!

I'm a friend of Evelyn, a member of your Advanced Reading team. She said she had spoken to you about my writing and that you had offered to give me some advice. I would really appreciate that as I've been submitting to agents but am considering going the indie route and would benefit from any insight you could offer me.

Rachel reread her paragraph at least ten times, still debating how to sign off and whether or not she had struck the right note. She didn't want to be presumptuous and send a manuscript right away. She added all the various ways the woman could contact her, including her phone number, and finally clicked send.

She immediately wished she could take it back. She shouldn't have included the phone number. The woman would think she was crazy. Who gives out their phone number?

Doing her breathing exercises again for another full two minutes helped her bring the panic back under control and she reasoned through the matter. Business people shared their numbers all the time. While it was true that she didn't have the filter of a secretary to field her calls, it was foolish to think the author would turn into a stalker. It was much more likely that she wouldn't contact Rachel by phone for fear of her being a stalker, not the other way around. It might have been better to not include her number, but it wasn't going to end up in an unsafe situation.

Jake messaging her would be an unsafe situation.

The thought popped into her head and wouldn't be dismissed. Rachel examined it from all angles. She didn't actually think Jake posed a threat to anything but her mental health. And that was only her own issues, not his. He hadn't shown any inclination to mock or torment. In fact, he had seemed quite contrite over startling her the two times they had come across one another. He even seemed to realize he hadn't been the best classmate in high school. Rachel had been relieved that he hadn't pursued the topic when it had come up as she didn't feel prepared to discuss it with him, but she was also happy to note that he was at least remotely aware that he might have harmed her in some way.

How was he to know that she felt lasting harm from her high school experience? Probably a more stable person wouldn't still be dealing with it some fifteen years later. Rachel really ought to find a new therapist. She had been seeing one off and on in Chicago but hadn't felt it had helped her overly. But now that she was embarking on a new life and both the closest source of anxiety and her dearest comfort were both gone, she could use some professional help to sort through her thoughts and feelings. And put away her multiple childhood traumas once and for all.

She knew it wouldn't be easy. But many worthwhile things weren't easy. Fixing up this beautiful house wasn't easy, but it was fulfilling. As was finishing a manuscript for the first time. That had been an intense amount of work, but the resulting pride of achievement was more than worth it. Rachel was reasonably sure that sorting out her mind would be just as worthwhile.

Rachel threw back the covers and finally got out of bed. She didn't quite have the enthusiasm for the day as she had experienced for a few heady days after that agent had requested her manuscript. But she had rebounded somewhat. Having a plan really helped her. She jotted down a couple notes about where she wanted her current story to go the next time she sat down to write. She also added a reminder to follow up with that previous client about the possibility of freelance work. It certainly wouldn't hurt her to get the ball rolling. And if she was going to try to stay here, it might be better to start drawing an income sooner rather than later.

The jingle of a notification on her phone accompanied her as she padded downstairs. Rachel was glad that Evelyn didn't seem to be in any sort of hurry to come over that morning as she was being slow about getting moving herself.

The jingle had been a message from Angela.

Hey girl, when are we going to share a bottle of wine again? Tina is ready whenever we are. Evenings are better for her, of course. And need time for babysitters. But it's her house this time. Next it will be yours <3

Rachel looked around her ripped apart main floor and shuddered. But it would be at least a week before she needed to worry about her friends seeing it. Besides, she assured herself, Evelyn had seen it and hadn't combusted from the horror. And in a week from now it could look like a completely different place.

But Rachel hadn't entertained in years. Really not ever. She and Todd hadn't been the dinner party type. Or Todd hadn't been anyway. Rachel didn't know. Maybe she would like to be the dinner party type. She actually laughed out loud at the thought. How did one get to be thirty-three years old and not know if she liked dinner parties? She gave her head a shake. She would research and plan one when the house was finished and find out how she felt about it.

Of course, hosting and attending were very different things. But it wouldn't really be cool to ask someone, 'hey, wanna have me over for a dinner party?' So, if she wanted to see what it was like, she'd have to do it herself. So far, girls' nights were fun. Not that she had hosted one yet. Maybe she shouldn't get too far ahead of herself. She would host the girls' night, see how that goes. If she survived and even enjoyed it, then she would think about the dinner party.

But should she invite Evelyn to girls' night?

Rachel bit her lip. What a conundrum. That was one of the other things she ought to already know by her ripe old age. How to juggle friendships.

There was a knock on her door that startled her out of her jumbled thoughts but also made her nearly jump out of her skin. She really needed to stop being so jumpy. It couldn't be good for her cardiovascular health.

Her hand flew to her head when she saw who was at her door.

"Jake, what are you doing here?" She didn't want to be self-conscious but despite the loathing she tried to muster up for the man, she couldn't ignore that he was one of the handsomest people she had ever seen in real life. There might be magazine models better looking, but it was likely they were airbrushed or something. There was nothing fake about Jake, not even the grin that stretched his face.

"Did I wake you up?" he asked, not seeming in the least repentant if he had.

"No, I was already awake, just not quite ready for my day yet."

"Sorry about that. I forget that most people don't start their day at 6:00, especially not here on the island."

Rachel didn't have an answer to that rejoinder, so she just nodded, keeping her eyebrows elevated to remind him he hadn't answered her question.

"Sorry, yes, why am I here was your question, right? Well, as I told you last night, I'm doing another job just down the lane a ways, so I thought it would be easier to just drop this off rather than emailing it to you."

"You thought stopping your car and coming and knocking on my door would be easier than clicking on a link in an email?" Rachel reframed to make sure she understood his crazy statement. It didn't seem to ruffle him in the least.

"Technology isn't my favorite thing. As I told you, we didn't all go to fancy universities."

"Perhaps not, but you aren't a total luddite, are you? If I remember correctly, you were really into computer games as a kid. That takes some tech-knowledge, doesn't it?"

"I have the required knowledge and understanding," he answered with a grin. "I just prefer face-to-face interaction."

"That's kind of weird," Rachel countered, surprised at her own brazenness.

Jake didn't seem to take offense, merely laughing at her words and shrugging. "I'm definitely not an introvert," he said amiably.

"I am," Rachel returned. "And I don't love surprises unless I've been warned."

Jake laughed again. "Then it's not a surprise."

"That's fine," she said with a smile.

"So, I suppose it's not your favorite thing to have someone show up unannounced."

"Not my favorite, no," she agreed, but she was surprising herself by growing more comfortable in his presence. "But since you know I wasn't expecting you, I suppose you can't have much in the way of expectations. At least I'm dressed, even if it's scruffy painting clothes." She nearly bit off her tongue. She shouldn't draw his attention to her state. She was a mess. She had pulled on the same clothes from yesterday but hadn't even combed her hair or washed her face. She had been too eager to get to the coffee pot. For all she knew, she could have raccoon eyes from smudged mascara that hadn't been properly removed the night before. She was desperate to check but didn't want him to think she was preening for him. Her stomach clenched even as she heard her voice saying the stupidest things. "Have you had your morning coffee yet? Or I suppose, if you've been running since 6:00 this is midmorning for you."

Jake grinned anew and Rachel couldn't decide if she wanted to push him out the door or pull him in further. She was having the oddest reactions that morning. Maybe this was a nightmare.

"I never say no to a cup of coffee. And I would love to see what you're doing with the place. I didn't ever get the chance to see the inside of this house, but I've always admired it."

"Don't you need to get to your worksite?" Rachel was regretting her polite offer already.

"Nah," Jake drawled. "My guys have it under control. I just need to check on them in a bit to make sure they don't have any questions for me."

Accepting that she had brought this calamity upon herself, and her only options were to accept it as gracefully as possible or to throw a fit and throw him out, Rachel stepped back and gestured him into her space.

"It'll take a minute to brew," she excused.

"I'm not in any rush," Jake assured her with a smile that Rachel was sure would turn a lesser woman inside out but only served to make her queasy.

She quickly went through the motions of setting the pot to brew, hoping she was doing it right because her brain was definitely not at its optimum.

"I'll be right back," she called as she dashed upstairs, leaving him to wander around the front room where he was checking out the view and the architecture. She wasn't comfortable leaving him to wander through her house, but she couldn't handle not knowing about her face. She would allow herself three minutes to run a comb through her hair and a face cloth over her features. If she could manage to slick on some mascara and lip gloss, she would consider it a win.

"That was fast," he remarked as he met her at the bottom of the stairs. "I like low maintenance women."

"I'm not low maintenance," she retorted.

He didn't argue, merely quirking an eyebrow as he glanced at her tied hair.

Rachel knew her face was revealing her embarrassment by coating her cheeks in hot pink, but she tried her best to ignore it with her chin elevated as she returned to the torn apart kitchen.

"I'm glad you aren't ripping everything out," Jake commented chattily behind her as she poured the coffee for them both. "Was that an esthetic choice or a budgetary one?"

"Both, I suppose you could say," Rachel answered with a bit of a sigh. "It still feels like I'm overstepping by doing anything to Aunt Eileen's house. But I love it almost exactly how it is. I just wanted to freshen it up a little bit. So, I'm not taking out any walls or making any major changes. Just fixing up some cracks here and there for the most part. But these cupboards just didn't seem to fit into the beach scene."

"Good choice. It seems they were much too dark for the rest of the house."

"Yeah. I don't know what she was thinking, to be honest. Nothing else in the whole house is like that."

"How did your aunt end up here? Is there some back story about the house?"

Rachel wrinkled her nose and shrugged. "I have no idea." Then she grimaced. "I probably should know, shouldn't I?" She sighed. "I was the worst niece in the history of family."

Chapter Eighteen

J ake raised his eyebrows at her words. "That's taking yourself a little seriously, isn't it?"

He hadn't meant to shock her, but for a beat she stared at him with her mouth ajar. It was kind of funny to him, but he didn't dare laugh. She was obviously serious about feeling badly about her relationship with her aunt.

Jake stared at her as she slowly shut her mouth and swallowed the retort that had obviously been on the tip of her tongue. It must have tasted bitter as her nose scrunched in the cutest way for a second.

"I suppose you're right. I am not the superlative here, am I?"

Jake scratched his head. "There you go again showing off your fancy education." He liked to emphasize a southern drawl when someone started using fancy words. Even though he was well-read now and no longer resented the grade he had failed in elementary school, he was still self-conscious of the fact that he didn't have a degree. He was confident enough in his own intelligence, but there was just something about Rachel that had always stirred him to reactions.

He had already admitted to himself that his treatment of her in school had stemmed from his discomfort with crushing on her, but what could be his excuse now? She was still beautiful, of course. Even more so than when she was a kid, in his opinion. There was a stillness about her that hadn't been there before. She used to be impetuous, quick to respond or react, definitely quick to be hurt. Now she hesitated and tested the situation before reacting. He liked that. There was evident maturity about her although she was still slim and hadn't shown any signs of aging despite the grief she was obviously feeling. He wondered if she'd had work done to be able to look so good. Fancy ladies in big cities often did that, according to his sister.

He was distracted from his spiraling thoughts by her sudden laughter. "Are you truly sensitive about my education? Or are you just teasing? I never understood teasing when we were in school, and I thought you were being mean to me all the time. But I am coming to understand as an adult that I might have been wrong."

"Well, I'm not all that sensitive about your education, just my lack thereof."

"Ah, I see," she said, her sharpened gaze making Jake want to squirm, but he managed to hold himself still.

Jake cleared his throat. "Anyhow, it looks like you've had experience refinishing furniture."

She laughed again. "Really? No, none. I just watched a bunch of videos online and then practiced on a scrap piece of wood until I was confident in my sanding abilities."

"That's pretty impressive, Rach. You could have a whole other career if you wanted it."

Adorably, she suddenly appeared bashful and couldn't meet his gaze. Again, Jake fought the urge to

163

hug the woman. He doubted she would welcome an embrace from him. He compromised with praise instead. "Your doors are coming out really well. I'm sure you'll be very happy with the end results. Just make sure you let them dry really good before you touch them to hang them back up. Once you have a couple coats on there, it takes longer to dry."

She nodded vigorously as though he had just confirmed what she thought. "And I think being right by the water affects it, too, right? Like there's more moisture in the air?"

"That's right. I suspect the salt in the air has something to do with it, too."

"Oh, that's interesting. And probably true. I will be sure to wait between coats. And wait a good long time before I try handling them. I would be so mad at myself if I wreck them after all this work."

"Well, it would still be fixable," Jake reminded her with a frown. It would seem the poor woman was very hard on herself. "I could stop by and help you hang them when you're ready."

"Oh no, I'm not ready to hire you."

Jake felt awkward. He hadn't even been thinking about money. He just wanted to spend a little time with her. For all her prickly awkwardness, he still found her appealing. But how was he to overcome her seeming rejection?

"I wasn't asking you for money; I was offering to help."

An expression he couldn't identify went across her face before he could figure it out. He was pretty sure she didn't know what to make of his offer, but he no longer thought she was necessarily trying to reject it. But she obviously felt awkward about accepting.

"Well, sure, if it doesn't take you away from your work too much. I would appreciate the help, as getting them off had been awkward enough. I had been thinking that Evelyn could help me, but you'd probably be even better."

She still sounded hesitant so he didn't push it, just leaving the offer in the open so she could accept when and if she wanted. Jake was reasonably sure from the looks of the doors she had a couple days of painting left at least before she could consider rehanging them. He would try to stop by before then to check on her progress and offer his help once more.

"What else do you plan to do in the house?" He turned the subject, which seemed to relieve her.

"Evelyn had a suggestion about how to get the grout in the bathroom clean. If that doesn't work, I'll be replacing the tiles in there. That will be my last big job. I feel like a wimp for hoping her suggestion works."

Jake laughed. "Not a wimp, just human. That's perfectly normal for anyone, but especially for someone new to home repairs," he assured her, hoping he didn't sound too earnest. "What was Evelyn's suggestion?"

"Baking soda."

Jake nodded. "That could work. If it doesn't, they have a really great product at the hardware store. I could lend you a tube of mine. You could try it on a spot and see if it works for you. If it does, you can get your own."

"Thanks," she seemed more pleased about an offer that didn't seem to her like charity. He would keep that in mind. "I would imagine that tiling would be a very big job."

"It is a big job and takes a fair bit of precision, depending on your surfaces and what kind of tile you picked out. It's not the best type of project for a newbie to take up."

"That's what I was afraid of, so I really hope either the baking soda or your product works." She paused for a moment and Jake started to wonder if he had overstayed his welcome, so he was surprised when she started to speak again. "To be honest, I never would have thought I would enjoy any sort of home projects like this. When I lived in Chicago, we had a brand new house that didn't need many things done to it to keep it up. I even had a housekeeper who came in once a week, so I didn't have to clean. So, this is a very different turn of events for me. But it turns out that I kind of like these projects. It's hard work but the sense of accomplishment when it turns out is kind of addictive."

Jake laughed and nodded. "And the more you do, the better you get, and the greater the high. It's kind of like a drug."

"Is that why you do it?" She actually looked open and eager to hear his answer. It was the first time he started to feel as though he could relax in her presence. He didn't want to get too used to it though. It wasn't likely she was ready to forgive him for the past.

"One of the reasons," he agreed. She looked as though she were going to ask him more questions, but he thought it would be better to leave her anticipating a future encounter. "I suppose I ought to get out of your hair since you weren't expecting me to stop by," he said reluctantly even though he knew it was the right thing to do. She didn't argue so he was even more convinced of that. Without much more interchange she escorted him to the door and waved him off.

Chapter Nineteen

R   achel could barely believe what had just happened.

She had exchanged conversation with Jake Callaghan. And enjoyed it. She had actually asked him questions. And looked forward to the answers. She was actually disappointed that he was leaving.

What was wrong with her??

Her stomach turned queasy as she overanalyzed the past fifteen minutes. Had she really combed her hair and put on makeup just because Jake had stopped by? Was she absolutely daft? Why would she do that? And why did she wish he hadn't left or that he would return again soon?

She was a glutton for punishment, that was why.

Her obsessive self-castigation was interrupted by another knock on the door at the same time as a jingle from her phone alerted her to an incoming message. Rachel was almost afraid to go see who it was trying to contact her on either source. She glanced quickly at the screen she pulled from her pocket. But there came another knock, so she made herself go to the door and was relieved to see Evelyn standing there holding a small basket.

"Sorry to leave you standing here," Rachel exclaimed as soon as she opened the door.

"Not at all. I figured you must have been involved in something or maybe you hadn't heard me."

Rachel thought about letting it go and not telling her why she hadn't come right away, but then she urged herself to be real with her friend. You have to be a friend to have friends, isn't that what the old adage says? If she wanted people to trust and confide in her, she would have to do the same, wouldn't she?

"Jake was here earlier so when I heard the knock, I didn't want to answer."

Evelyn stared at her with widened eyes. "Is he still here?" she whispered, sounding torn between excited and scandalized.

"No," Rachel retorted hotly. "That wasn't why I didn't want to answer. I was afraid it might be him coming back."

"Oh." Evelyn sounded disappointed. "That's far less juicy," she said with a laugh. "Did something happen? Are you ok? Do I need to take my broom to him?"

Now Rachel joined her in laughing. "No, no, he didn't do anything untoward. It was a perfectly pleasant exchange. But I can't be comfortable with perfectly pleasant exchanges with Jake Callaghan."

By now, Rachel had realized that the basket Evelyn was holding held freshly baked muffins, and her stomach reminded her that she hadn't yet eaten anything with its loud grumbling. With a laugh they adjourned into the front room, and each broke open a muffin.

"Thank you so much for these, Ev. But I should be feeding you as a thank you for your help, not the other way around."

"Not at all." Evelyn waved away Rachel's words. "But tell me everything. Why can't you be comfortable? Is it still the something you didn't want to talk about from high school?"

Rachel sighed and nodded. "I can't decide if he was evil as a boy and changed somehow or if maybe I have it all wrong and have built it up into something it's not in the past fifteen years."

Evelyn smiled around her bite of muffin. "I don't think evil boys turn into sweet and hunky men."

"You shouldn't be calling him hunky; you're married."

"I might be married and thoroughly devoted to my husband, but I still have eyes in my head."

"He is hunky," Rachel agreed glumly, making Evelyn giggle.

"If you hire him for the pier, you'll have all sorts of eye candy for the time of the project."

"But I don't know if I can stand the tumult he causes me."

"Did you ever think you should maybe talk to him about whatever transpired between you so long ago?"

"And admit that he has that kind of power over me? Wouldn't it be better for me to find a therapist and work it out that way?"

Evelyn laughed again. "I vote for doing both. Obviously, you have some hang-ups you would benefit from a little time in therapy to deal with. But whether Jake sees the situation the same way as you do or not, clearly you've been scarred by your experiences from back then. Maybe talking to him about it might help you move on from it."

Rachel didn't anticipate that it would be at all an enjoyable conversation, but if he was going to come around, she couldn't not talk to him about it. Or she could just find a realtor and leave. Rachel didn't think she could face such a conversation. There weren't enough therapy sessions in the world for her to be able to revisit those painful memories. But she found herself promising Evelyn she would at least think about it.

Turning the subject, Rachel asked Evelyn how her husband took the topic of fostering or adopting, but it quickly turned the mood dark.

Evelyn sighed. "I still didn't talk to him about it. He was home so late last night; I didn't want to risk spoiling the mood and then having him have to stay up too late hashing it out."

"Well, aren't we a pair?" Rachel commented with a twist of her lips. "But at least you have baking to pour your feelings into."

Evelyn smiled. "It centers me, for sure."

"So, tell me, Evelyn. Do you plan to be a stay-at-home mom?"

It was exactly the right question to ask. Evelyn grinned and nodded. "For at least a little while. But I'm hoping to be able to come up with some sort of home-based business so that I could help out with our finances a little but still be home with the kids."

"What a brilliant idea. Do you know what sort of business you might do?"

Evelyn shook her head and shrugged.

"Well, I've been looking at freelancer websites lately. That might give you some ideas of somewhere to start. It seemed to me like you could do anything on a freelance basis. That's not quite the same as starting a business. But it's somewhere to start."

"Thanks, Rachel, I'll look into that. And if you talk to Jake and get over your discomfort and stay here, then we can be work-from-home buddies."

Rachel had hoped Evelyn would forget about Jake, but she laughed along with her anyway. "Sounds fun," she said, sounding a bit limp. To cover it up she clapped and rubbed her hands together. "Who's ready for another coat of paint?"

Evelyn laughed. "I would say your doors are. But I'm ready to add it."

"Are you sure?" Rachel asked, despite the fact that she had brought it up. "Are you certain this won't hurt you in some way and compromise your chances?"

"I'm very sure. For one thing, you bought the good, low odor kind of paint so that's no problem. For another, having something to do will keep my mind off my worries. I'm very sure I want to help you. For one more thing, I want you to stay. So, if I can help you get attached to the house to the point where you don't want to leave, it's in my best interests."

Rachel laughed along with her friendly neighbor. "Well, I'm already very attached to the house, so you needn't worry there."

"Well then, I want you to be able to do whatever you want to do and not have to worry about projects. I don't know what I would have done if I had to do it all myself when we were doing our house."

"Well, it looked to me like you did a major rebuild of your house. This project isn't the same thing at all."

"Maybe not, but I'm very happy to help." And she suited her words to actions, grabbing a roller and getting things started. "Now tell me about your search for some freelance work."

"Actually, just before you knocked, I got an email notification but didn't read it yet."

"From who?" Evelyn puzzled even as she started rolling the paint onto the doors.

"From that old client I used to work for. I think I mentioned them when we were talking about my job search the last time. I think they would be perfect for needing a freelance accountant. There might be a few

171

extra busy times like tax season but other than that, I think just one day each week would be all they'd need me for. But as their former accountant, I know they are in a position to pay me well."

Both women laughed and kept on with their painting. Companionable silence descended between them for a time.

The rest of the day flew by for Rachel. Evelyn stayed and helped with the rest of the second coat on the cupboards and doors, but it went even faster than the day before. She seemed reluctant to leave but it was evident she also didn't want to overstay her welcome.

"Will you be doing another coat tomorrow?" she'd asked almost eagerly as she was going out the door.

"Jake mentioned we ought to be very careful that the coats dry in between. He said that being right by the water could make them take longer. So, I think it might be better to wait two days. I expect the third coat will be the last."

Evelyn giggled. "You're taking Jake's advice now, are you?"

She didn't bother to await an answer Rachel didn't have. She skipped down the steps giggling like a little girl.

Well, at least someone is getting amusement out of this, Rachel thought with a shake of her head. Because she suspected she might be losing her mind.

She was on a wild ride at this point in her life, but Rachel was determined to hold on with both hands. At least there were many positive things besides the sorrow. That thought reminded her of one of the exercises that had been recommended in one of her mindset groups – counting her blessings.

She wasn't homeless. That was certainly a bonus and had been a very real possibility if she had remained in Chicago. Of course, if Aunt Eileen was alive, she would have welcomed Rachel to stay with her one way or the other. That would have been a very different experience, of course. And Rachel might have been too proud or independent to accept. And now she was all the way off track from her plan to count her blessings and was getting upset.

Rachel took a moment for some breathing exercises to get her rioting emotions back under control and started again.

New and old friends was another thing to be thankful for. But where would she put Jake on that list? Would she put Jake on that list? He was being friendly, but he was certainly not an old friend, despite what he might think.

Rachel took more deep breaths and worked hard to keep her focus on her blessings, not getting derailed once more.

A plan. She was ridiculously grateful that she had a plan. Since the death of her parents, Rachel had never been comfortable if there weren't contingency plans in place for every possible outcome. She now had a few when weeks ago, even days ago, she had feared she would be aimless for the rest of her life.

She would be able to keep working in a field that she had loved while also trying out a new venture that she suspected she might love even more.

That was enough to buoy her back up, and she was excited to pursue those last two items. Evelyn's writer friend had sent a long email with several suggestions. But she had also offered to read a sample of her work and offer a critique.

The thought of the critique made her belly clench with anxiety, but Rachel knew it would be helpful. She needed an experienced eye to tell her whether or not it was any good. Aunt Eileen had been more than supportive, but her good opinion might have been slightly biased.

Rachel grinned remembering the last time they had discussed one of her stories.

"You have the most unique turn of phrase, Rachel dear. And you somehow manage to keep me guessing about the story. Which is amazing, considering how well I know you, and we even discuss your stories."

They had laughed and then exchanged a few innocuous anecdotes about their days and said goodbye. That had been their last conversation. But it had been a good one.

The memory warmed Rachel. She hadn't been able to remember conversations with Eileen like that in her grief. The fact that she could actually hear her aunt in her head felt like a little gift or a reward for her hard work. It brought tears to her eyes, but Rachel suspected they were of joy not grief.

She went off to her laptop to respond to both the accountancy message and the authorly one with the light of joy lighting up her evening.

Chapter Twenty

And then two days passed.

Rachel had to avail herself of her breathing exercises more times than she wanted to count. She hadn't heard back from either the author or the possible freelance company. Both had seemed so eager to communicate with her at first.

Did that mean the chapters she had sent over were dreadful? Did the company no longer wish to work with her? She was grumbling to herself and agonizing over the thoughts when Evelyn arrived with a grin and a basket, as usual. Even that somehow irritated Rachel, but she tried not to let it show.

She was not successful.

"Aw, honey, are you having a bad morning?" Evelyn asked with concern. "Should I come back or help you power through?" She didn't wait for an answer, simply bustling in and making herself at home. "Have you eaten yet? I had thought to save these muffins for a coffee break mid-morning, but if you need a pick me up now, you're welcome to them."

"No, I'm fine, we can get started."

Even to Rachel's ears she sounded as belligerent as a rebellious teenager. It didn't help when she saw Evelyn's lips twitching as though she were amused by her. The only good thing was that Rachel's anger propelled her through the morning almost like nervous energy, and she got more work done faster than usual. Evelyn was productive too, since they weren't chatting as much as they normally did. Before they realized it, all the painting was finished. At least, what they had planned to do that morning. It helped that they had decided the cupboards themselves didn't need a third coat, only the doors.

Sitting back on her heels, Rachel admired their work.

"This was terrific, Evelyn, thank you so much. And we didn't even stop for a break, so now we can relax with our muffins and coffees, and you can take your time berating me for being a grouch."

"I would never do that." Evelyn sounded appalled at the very thought, which lightened Rachel's mood even more than getting the painting finished had done.

"I know, I was just joking. But I deserve it so if you want to try, please go ahead."

"Of course not. But if you want to talk about it, I'm all ears."

Rachel grinned at the expression as she fussed with the coffee maker. She would be glad to have the kitchen restored to full usefulness. Living out of boxes was a pain that she wouldn't miss. One more reason why she was upset she hadn't heard from either the client or Evelyn's author friend, but what could she do? If she harassed them with more messages, they would be even less likely to want to work with her.

Finally, they sat down outside with their steaming cups and threw blankets over their legs.

"I love sitting out here even though it would make much more sense to stay inside."

"Inside is fine, but the view is even better from here," Evelyn agreed. "And out here you can hear the surf."

"It never gets old, does it?"

Evelyn smiled and nodded but didn't allow the subject to turn. "So, what's going on with you?"

Rachel turned to her with a sheepish expression. "I'm truly sorry for being such a bear today. I've been stressing, which leads to not sleeping well. That's no excuse, merely an explanation."

"No apologies are necessary, we're friends, I promise. But why are you so stressed? Has something happened?"

"It's more that nothing has happened. When you were here the other day, I had received emails from both that author you read for and the company I'm hoping to do some accounting for. So, I messaged them both as soon as you left. And then it has been crickets ever since."

Evelyn stared at her. "But that was just two days ago."

"They seemed eager enough at first," Rachel grumbled.

Evelyn smiled. "Well, I can answer one of the problems. Catherine is at a conference or writing retreat or something. I've forgotten the exact details, but I follow her online, and she was talking about it. She's been talking about it for weeks actually, so I should be a little better informed," she concluded with a grimace. "But whichever it is, she probably doesn't have any time to read what you sent her, and she doesn't want to write you back until she does. And it has only been two days," she repeated, making Rachel laugh.

"I know, I know. But I was so excited."

"Well, you should still be excited," Evelyn prodded. "It has only been two days."

Now they were both laughing, and Rachel nodded.

"You're right. Thank you. And thank you for that extra insight. I suppose, even without being away, two days might not be enough time for her to have gotten to it, depending on how busy she is. I am just so anxious for her response that it feels much longer."

"I know, sweetie. But I'm sure as soon as she's back, she'll get right on it. Maybe she'll even read it on the plane or something. Was it a very long passage you sent her?"

"No, just the first three chapters."

"Well then, she should be able to read through that pretty quick, I would think."

Rachel nodded. "I'm not too sure what goes into a critique. Maybe she's marking it all up."

"How would you feel about that?" Evelyn asked.

With a sigh, Rachel answered. "Well, I want to say I would appreciate her taking the time. But I'm not going to lie and say I'm excited to receive criticism."

"I don't think critique necessarily means criticism. She talks about her critique meetings all the time in her posts, and she sounds like she really enjoys them."

"She's also an experienced, successful author," Rachel countered drily. "But you're right, I need to stop borrowing trouble. There are any number of reasons why she hasn't sent me any messages, and not all of them mean she hated my chapters."

"Exactly," Evelyn agreed with a light laugh. "Now tell me what else seems to be troubling you. I feel like there was more to it than just those things."

"Those were pretty big things," Rachel countered.

"Mmm hmm, they were, but still," Evelyn prompted, leading to Rachel heaving another sigh.

"All right. It's Jake."

"What about him?" Evelyn demanded, heat rising in her voice. "Did he hurt you again? Do I need to track him down and have some words?"

Rachel was stunned silent for a moment, but then giggles erupted from her. "No, no, he didn't do anything except be nice. He offered to help me hang the doors back up when they're ready to go."

Evelyn stared at her as though waiting for more. When Rachel didn't have anything else to say, she gestured a beckoning motion. "And what else?"

Rachel shrugged. "Nothing else. I just don't know what to do with a nice Jake. I had him painted as the villain from my entire childhood. And now I'm left wondering if he could have changed that much or if I imagined the whole thing."

Evelyn wrinkled her nose. "It's possible the truth is somewhere in the middle."

"Yeah, not just possible but maybe even probable," Rachel agreed. "But it's messing with my head."

"Are you going to talk to him about it?"

"I don't know. Do you think I should? He'll probably think I'm crazy."

"If that's the case, then you won't be any further behind, at least. If he isn't going to be a good friend to you, you don't need him in your life. If he thinks you're crazy, maybe he'll give you a wide berth. Or he'll explain himself, and you'll have your backstory straightened out."

Rachel nodded in agreement, but she didn't know if she would ever be able to follow through on Evelyn's suggestion whether it had merit or not.

"Tell me about your week, besides painting," Rachel prompted. "That's one thing I miss about working in an office. I'm not the most outgoing person, but I do enjoy hearing other people's business. In a

179

large office, there was always drama to observe from other people. If I do stay here and find remote work to do, I'm going to have to develop a circle of sorts."

"Well count me in your circle, but I don't have anything too exciting to tell you. We have an appointment with the fertility doctor coming up next week, and I'm working on breathing through the anxiety and excitement."

"You do breathing exercises, too?" Rachel asked, embarrassed about how excited she was to hear that. "Which is your favorite?"

"I haven't picked a favorite," Evelyn laughed. "Do you have one?"

"Absolutely! Box breathing is the best thing that was ever introduced to me."

"I don't know if I'm familiar with that one or maybe it's called something different by our clinic."

"You breathe in for the count of three, hold for the count of three, breathe out for the count of three, then hold for the count of three once more. I don't know what it is about that pattern. Maybe it's the counting and the little number cruncher in my head loves that. But it never fails to pull me out of a spiral when I need it."

"I'll keep that in mind," Evelyn answered with a smile.

"Do you need company for your appointment?"

Evelyn reached out and clasped her hand. "Thank you so very much for the offer, but no, I'll be going with my husband, so I should totally be fine. In fact, he's taken the day off and we're planning to make a whole day of it and turn it into a date." Evelyn sighed softly. "It has been so long since we've done something like that. Despite how anxious I am about the appointment itself, I really can't wait for the day to get here."

"That does sound fun. I'm glad Eric has planned to support you like that. I think it's a team effort even though you'll be the one carrying the baby."

"I have to say, Rachel, I really adore how positive you are about this."

Heat flooded through Rachel, and she instantly wondered if she ought to be less excited for her neighbor to get pregnant. "I'm sorry, should I be more even-keeled on the topic?"

"Not in the least. I promise, I wasn't implying anything. I genuinely appreciate your positivity, especially considering you aren't always positive about some subjects."

Rachel laughed. She couldn't argue with that statement. She could be Negative Nancy at times, for sure. She shrugged.

"I just really feel this time it's going to work for you. You are definite mom material."

Evelyn got to her feet. "I suppose I ought to head home and get supper on the go." She headed for the door but then turned back with a sly expression. "Are you going to let Jake know that we've finished?"

"No, I'm going to wait and see how they look once they're dry. Maybe they'll need another coat."

"They don't need another coat; you just don't want to risk having the handsome handyman in your house."

Rachel laughed and shrugged. "There might be an element of that thrown in the mix."

Evelyn went out the door with a wave and a promise to be in touch.

Rachel headed for her keyboard. She felt the urge to clean the house but didn't want to stir up any dust that might stick in her fresh coat of paint. She was also well aware that the urge to clean was merely a procrastination measure, and she had no wish to follow through on that. She could at least get a little more work done while she obsessed over her employment situation.

The day flew by. If anyone had told her in the past that she would one day enjoy days without structure she would never have believed. But Rachel was enjoying being the queen of her own life. While she did enjoy structure, she was confident she would be able to create it for herself as needed. For now, she was still coming to terms with her losses and needed to figure out where she was going with her life more conclusively before she defined exactly how it was going to look.

She was also excited to visit with Angela and Tina again. Much more than she would have expected. Looking through her closet, the next afternoon, though, Rachel was forced to roll her eyes. She had no "in between" clothes. She had professional clothes, even some formal attire, and she had really old clothes that she found appropriate for her renovation projects. She really didn't have many "hanging out with girlfriends" clothes.

Finally, after pulling out nearly everything that used to hang in her closet, Rachel had cobbled together an outfit that she felt would pass muster.

Rachel tried to tell herself that friends ought to accept her how she was, and she was a professional who dressed accordingly. But maybe that was becoming less true. Maybe she might one day be a jeans sort of woman. Stranger things had happened.

She grinned at her reflection as she finished applying her makeup and fluffing her hair. She didn't look dreadful.

"Girl, you look amazing," Angela greeted her as she opened the door to the modern townhouse. "How do you manage that?"

Rachel laughed and shrugged. She didn't necessarily agree with her friend, but she wasn't going to decline the compliment.

"Come in here, you two," Tina demanded from the back of the house. Or the front.

"What do you call this part of your house?" she asked Tina as soon as they convened in the kitchen.

Angela laughed but Tina stared at her as though she were an idiot. "This room with all the appliances? Most people would call it a kitchen." Sarcasm dripped from every syllable.

Rachel laughed even as her cheeks heated. "Not that," she said. "I've been wondering which is the front and the back of the house. In a traditional city-like setting, the street side of your house is the front, and then you have a backyard. Angela's house is like that. But with your house and mine, the beach is our backyard. But it feels like that ought to be considered the front as it's so beautiful. I keep having this conversation with myself."

"You have conversations with yourself?" Tina asked, still with the sarcasm.

"Cut it out, Tina," Angela said gently. "We agreed to be friendly and welcoming."

Feeling awkward, Rachel tried to laugh. "You agreed to be friendly and welcoming to me? As in, you had to debate the topic?"

"Not like that," Angela assured her. "It's just that I was so excited when I heard you were back in town and told Tina, she –"

"Stow it, Angela," Tina interrupted.

"I'm sorry. I have no intention of coming between the two of you," Rachel stammered out, even as she wondered what sort of a weird relationship she had stepped into. To her shock, both women stared at her and laughed.

"Not like that, silly," Angela said, even as Tina suddenly relaxed, put down the knife she had been using to prepare a platter of something, and hurried around the counter to pull Rachel into a hug.

"I'm sorry, Rachel. Angela is right, I am being a grouch. And we HAD agreed to try to be friendly. It just takes way more effort for me than it does for Angela." She sighed and stepped back to her counter again. "I interrupted Angela just now because she was going to tell you my personal business, and my standard attitude is prickly pear at all times, so I instinctively wanted her to stop. But in the spirit of being friends and all, you ought to know that my divorce just became final this week."

"Oh no, Tina, I'm so sorry." Rachel meant it. No matter what she had stepped into, she didn't wish that sort of upheaval and unhappiness onto anyone. Her own messy life was evidence enough for her that she needed to offer empathy or understanding or at least give the benefit of the doubt wherever possible.

"Not your fault," Tina continued briskly. "You weren't his secretary, were you?"

Rachel laughed awkwardly but didn't say anything else. It filled her with guilt to feel this way, but the fact that the other woman's life wasn't nearly as perfect as it looked at first glance was a relief and made her feel much more open to forming a friendship with her. She chewed her lip.

"You're thinking about quitting on us, aren't you?" Tina now challenged.

"Quitting on you? What do you mean?"

"Now that it's evident I'm no longer the perfect teenager," Tina said defiantly.

Rachel shook her head. "The exact opposite, as a matter of fact. I feel like a horrible person and didn't want to admit this to you, but the fact that you

184

AREN'T the perfect little cheerleader anymore is actually much more inviting, since my life is such a hot mess. I felt like a fraud being here with the two of you with your perfect lives and perfect husbands and children."

Both women exchanged a quick glance and laughed long and loud. Finally, Tina grinned at Rachel. "Angela's life might be nearly perfect, but mine is far from it. You are welcome in our little club just as you are. But now that you've brought it up, here's a glass of wine, there's a seat," she said gesturing to one of the stools at the kitchen island, "and start spilling."

"Wait," Angela interrupted, "you still didn't say whether this is the front or the back of the house."

They all laughed again, and Rachel finally felt herself relax into their company. Maybe it wasn't so dreadful that she was relieved to see their lives weren't so very perfect. Not to say that misery loves company, but it would be hard to live up to if hers was the only messy life.

"I'm a traditionalist, despite most appearances," Tina said. "So, I can understand fully why you think the street side is the front of the house. But especially on this island, on the beach side, even architecturally, the houses look like the front is facing the ocean. And if I remember correctly, your street isn't really a street. At most it's a glorified lane. So, I vote beachside is the front. So front door, front porch, beach side."

"I agree," Angela stated firmly, making them all laugh again.

"Now spill it, Rachel." And with Tina's firm command, Rachel found herself spilling her confusion about Jake.

"And so, he has quoted on doing some work for me, and according to my neighbor, he's the only one who qualifies to do the major project I have left to do. I've been hesitating over it because I'm not sure if I'll be staying. Or rather, at first, I wasn't sure if I would want to stay. And Jake is the main reason for that."

"So, what you're saying is that all of your problems come back to Jake," Tina summed it up dramatically making Rachel blush and Angela throw a handful of popcorn at her.

"That's a massive over simplification," Rachel declared irritably.

"Perhaps, but it made us all laugh," Tina argued. "But seriously, Rachel, that's a lot. I'm glad you're more seriously considering staying here, but I'm surprised Jake holds so much power over that decision. And why would you even consider hiring him in that case? But also, why are you letting a little teenaged crush affect you to this day?"

"It wasn't such a little crush. He tormented me for years."

Both women stared at her. "I thought you guys liked each other when we were kids," Tina finally said with a frown. "I mean, I know you never actually went out and you left as soon as school was over, but he was really devastated when you just walked out on him."

Rachel's jaw nearly hit the floor. "I walked out on him? What are you talking about? He and his friends mocked me every single day of our school life together. I'm amazed I enjoyed learning so much with what a tough experience it was for me in those years."

Even Angela was shaking her head with a frown. "Wow, Rachel. That's so fascinating. I really should have finished my psych degree; I might know how to explain this. But it would seem that you both had the same experience from very different viewpoints. I think he had a crush on you and was such a guy that he didn't know how to express it. And maybe he feared your rejection or something and thus acted out. I'm so sorry that it affected you so strongly, and I'm not saying that it was right how he acted, but I'm pretty certain it wasn't malicious in nature."

"I'm not one who's big on communication, but even I'm going to say you ought to talk to him about it." Tina's words lightened the mood, and they all laughed a little.

"Evelyn, my neighbor, said the same thing. But I think maybe a part of me is afraid that all my inner demons will turn out to be simply brought on by my own imagination if it turns out that I was wrong all those years ago."

Angela put her arm around Rachel. "It doesn't really matter if Jake's intentions were malicious or not if they hurt you that badly. That part is very real, and its impact on you all the more so." She paused for a moment before adding in a hesitant voice, "Is it possible that it was just really dreadful timing? You were probably entering puberty when you lost both your parents. A too smart, grieving child was thrust into a classroom full of equally hormonal strangers. No one knew how to deal with feelings. You no longer had a father figure who could explain teen boys and their stupid behavior. Who knows what Jake might have been going through at the time?"

Tina piped up. "I know he hated being older than the rest of us since he flunked the sixth grade, then this pretty little girl comes into the class smarter than everyone else. Do you think that might have played a part?"

Rachel nodded and sighed. "Everything makes so much sense through the lens of being a grown up."

Angela kept her arm around Rachel and squeezed her shoulders as she almost whispered her next question. "I hesitate to ask this, but why didn't your aunt help you deal with it?"

Rachel stared out past her friends to the rolling surf that was barely visible through the big window in the growing darkness. She sighed heavily.

"I never told her. I was so wrapped up in my grief and anger. I didn't know how to talk about it. And I suppose she was deeply grieving, too. My dad was her only living relative besides me. They were really close."

"And she was never married?" Tina asked, despite the quelling look she received from Angela.

"No. I feel badly, but I never asked her why she didn't. I was too wrapped up in my own drama for a long time, so didn't think to ask. Then I didn't want to talk about my own situation and feared it would come up if we got talking about marriage, so I fell back onto the very healthy psychological crutch of avoidance," she concluded with sarcastic humor, lightening the suddenly heavy mood.

"That's all a lot, Rachel," Angela commented with sympathy. Rachel nodded.

"Yeah," she agreed. "But who doesn't have stuff, right?"

Tina laughed and lifted her hand, waving it. "I'm definitely in that club."

"I really hope you can put this stuff behind you, though, Rachel. You're obviously an intelligent woman. And we quite like you. You'd be an asset to the island. But also, I hate to see you suffering like this," Angela said. Tina rolled her eyes at her friend but nodded along with her. Rachel felt warm inside her heart for the first time in ages. Maybe since she was thirteen and had lost her parents.

Living in her aunt's house and feeling that Eileen had loved her until the end had restored her foundation, but gaining friends for the first time in years was restoring her confidence. She could do this life thing.

"I'm planning to stay. So, I suppose I ought to do that project at some point. And that means dealing with Jake, so I suppose I'll have to talk to him. If he doesn't say the right things, I'll just fire him and ignore him for the rest of my life," she concluded with a laugh and a shrug.

"That's the spirit," Tina chortled, passing the plate of cheese and crackers. "Now, eat up."

The rest of the evening passed quickly, and Rachel soon found herself back at home, sleeping deeply with a smile upon her face.

Chapter Twenty-One

I t was the first time she could remember ever bounding out of bed full of energy. Probably as a child that had happened, of course, especially here in this house when her family would visit in the summers. But as an adult, Rachel had always felt getting out of bed to be a struggle. Not that morning.

She was ready to face the day. A glance at the clock told her she was much earlier than usual. She decided to start the day with a brisk walk on the beach. That would allow her to plot out what she wanted to write that day and might also extend the energetic streak.

Rachel had been right. She was soon back in her cozy little office pounding out her words on the keyboard, deeply immersed in her story. She was so caught up in her characters that she almost didn't notice the knocking on the back door. With a frown, she realized it wasn't coming from her imagination. With a laugh, she realized she had almost written it into her story.

She quickly hit the save button and hurried from the room.

"Jake!" she exclaimed when she opened the door.

"I know, I really need to start messaging you before turning up at your door, I'm sorry," he apologized immediately, looking mussed and sheepish even in all his handsome glory.

That day he was wearing old worn jeans that seemed like they'd seen better days, but they were still clean and crisp as though he had pulled them from the drawer only recently. His similarly aged T-shirt hugged his muscles as though made just for him. Rachel had to work not to stare.

"Have I caught you at a bad time? Perhaps I should just make an appointment," he added. Rachel realized he sounded nervous. He was almost babbling.

"Sorry, no, it's fine, I was just in the middle of a thought, and my brain is having trouble catching up to what's happening now."

He nodded even though he appeared puzzled by her words. "Were you thinking about hanging your doors today or tomorrow? I thought I could help you, if you haven't done it yet."

Rachel grinned and stepped back. "I took your advice about the paint needing to dry thoroughly, very seriously, so no, they haven't been hung yet. Come in." She gestured. "I just need to write one thing down and then I'll be back." Without further explanation, she ran back to her office just to make a note of where she had meant to take the story. She hated to cut off in the middle of a thought and didn't want to lose it.

She thought about dealing with her appearance but didn't want to make him think she was primping for his benefit. A quick glance in a mirror as she passed it reminded her that she had actually combed her hair that morning and put on a touch of makeup. She might not be glamorous, but she didn't look the worst ever.

"Sorry about that, I was just in the middle of a paragraph and needed to write down where I had planned to go with the rest of the chapter," she excused breathily as she ran back down the stairs.

Jake stared at her. "Are you writing a story?"

Heat flooded her cheeks. It was becoming such a part of her life that she forgot it wasn't the norm for most people.

"I am," she nodded.

"Have you written anything else? Are you published?"

"You sound like you know a little bit about publishing," she commented.

Jake shrugged. "Not really. I think nearly everyone claims to want to write a book, but very few ever do it. I once dated a woman who was trying to get into publishing. But she could never finish the story, so it didn't go anywhere. Through her, though, I learned a little bit about it."

Rachel nodded and chose to ignore the niggle of what seemed like jealousy that ate at her when he mentioned someone he had dated. How ridiculous, she scoffed at herself. "It's true about everyone wanting to write but few actually following through. And it's true that finishing the thing seems to somehow be the hardest part. Of course, I've never yet had an editor, so that part might actually end up being harder, but for me, it took many tries before I was finally able to complete an entire manuscript."

She tried not to preen under the admiring expression on his face.

"That's awesome, Rach. What do you write?"

"Oh, I forgot to mention, though, that nothing has yet been published. I'm still querying agents." She fidgeted from nerves. It was still an awkward topic for her. "But in answer to your question, so far everything I've written has been historical fiction set in Regency era England."

Jake's eyebrows rose. "That must take so much research."

She lifted a shoulder and one side of her mouth followed it in a lopsided smile. "Yeah, it does," she agreed. "But remember, I'm a geek, so I enjoy it."

"I never said you were a geek, I said you were a brainiac. There's a difference."

Rachel laughed but saw her opportunity to bring up the tricky subject of the past. She hesitated to do it but then took a deep breath and plunged in. "I'm not sure you knew the difference back in high school."

That wiped the smile of his face, and her stomach clenched. She shouldn't have brought it up. But she stood her ground and didn't take it back.

"No, I probably did know the difference," Jake began hesitantly, no longer able to hold her gaze. "But I was an idiot in more ways than one."

She still had the very strong urge to undo what she had done by bringing up the topic, but she didn't want to let him off the hook that easily, and she knew her friends were right, she probably did need to have this awkward conversation for her own well-being, especially if she wanted to stay on the island. Rachel took a deep breath.

"Why?" she asked. "Why did you feel the urge to mock someone who wasn't equipped to defend herself?"

"Besides the aforementioned idiocy?" he asked, looking adorably sheepish and bashful.

Rachel actually felt an urge to comfort him, but she really needed to know the answer. She lifted one shoulder once again and nodded. "Like, specifically, why? Was I particularly offensive to you in some way? Or do I recall it incorrectly, and you were beastly to everyone, and I only thought it was just me?"

Jake stared at her and his face flushed with hot color. Rachel wondered if he was getting angry as he glanced at the door as though wishing he hadn't come in. Finally, he took a deep breath and let it out slowly. First, he mirrored her one shouldered shrug and then lifted his hands almost helplessly.

"You were the cutest little thing I had ever seen when you walked into our classroom with your pink top that matched your sneakers and your hair in braids all the way down your back."

Rachel's mouth fell open. "You thought I was cute?" she scoffed. "No way!"

"Teenaged boys can be total dolts, surely you realize," he said with an uncomfortable sounding laugh. "But then you turned out to be smarter than everyone else, and I was jealous besides."

"Besides what?"

"Besides having a little crush on you."

"You couldn't have had a crush on me." Rachel rejected the idea, and he shrugged again.

"I could and I did."

"But you treated me horribly," she objected.

"I know, and I'm truly sorry for that. I know it even got worse in our final year, but by then some of it was habit. I also was worried that I'd never see you again, and I was angry that I had blown my chance with you."

"No," Rachel said it softly at first, but then repeated it more strongly as she shook her head. "No, that's not how you treat someone when you like them. I refuse to believe that. I deserve better treatment."

"Of course, you do," Jake agreed instantly with a frown creasing his forehead as Rachel continued to shake her head and tears began to form in her eyes.

"I deserve better," she repeated.

"You do, absolutely. You did back then, and you do today." He stared at her helplessly. "Is there anything I can say or do that can make it up to you even a little bit?"

Rachel opened her mouth but had nothing to say. She sat down suddenly on the nearest seat, a beat up old wooden chair that she had been using as a ladder, so it was liberally coated with paint splashes, but she didn't care. She absently gestured for him to take a seat, too.

"I'm surprised you haven't kicked me out of your house and off your property," Jake added when she didn't answer his question.

Finally, after another moment of awkward silence, Rachel looked at him. "I don't mean to beat you up after you've apologized, and this might sound melodramatic, but your treatment of me kind of blighted my life."

He paled before her eyes but didn't run screaming from the house. He waited in silence as though knowing she had more to say.

"My friends have told me that maybe I've misremembered or that there was more to it than just what I saw on the surface. I guess they were right in a way." Rachel ran a hand through her hair and looked out the window. "The hilarious-slash-sad thing is that I kind of had a little crush on you, too. At first, anyway. You kind of squashed that as time went by."

Color ebbed and flowed on his face as she spoke, but he continued to hold his silence, merely watching her with what appeared to be an attempt at openness on his face, as though he wanted to allow her to tell him exactly how she felt. Rachel surprised herself with a watery laugh.

"You have certainly turned into a good listener," she said, which made his color deepen, and he shrugged again.

"I think I told you about my niece."

"Ah, yes, that's right."

"It's actually because of her that I'm even more ashamed of my treatment of you," Jake added. "I would feel inclined to kill anyone who pulled the same with her. I'm actually surprised no adults ever intervened on your behalf."

Rachel nodded. "Yeah, I should have told someone. It might have helped us both."

"You never told anyone? Why not?"

Rachel put her chin in her hand as her elbow leaned on the nearby table, suddenly feeling as though her head was too heavy. "I was going through a lot, I guess. Where would I have started? And who would I have told? The cutest boy in school treated me like something he found under his shoe. At thirteen and grieving, there wasn't anything I could do with all that angst."

"Ugh! Rachel," he exclaimed, reaching across the table to take her hand. "I'm truly, intensely sorry. I wish I could take it back."

Rachel allowed him to squeeze her hand before she offered him a wobbly smile and withdrew her hand from his grasp slowly. "I wish you could, too. But talking about it has actually helped. And I need to accept the responsibility for my reactions and my silence. You're right, I could have and should have told someone. If I hadn't felt like I could tell Eileen, I should have talked to one of the guidance counselors or something. And I shouldn't have allowed it to keep me away from the only home I had left."

Jake's face paled again. "That's why you never came back? Because of me?"

"Quite dramatic, isn't it?" she asked with an embarrassed laugh. "But don't let it go to your head," she admonished. "It wasn't just you by the end of school. It was half the class. And really, the teachers should have known. And they never should have picked me to be the valedictorian."

"You had the highest grades," Jake objected. "Probably by quite a large margin. It wasn't a matter of picking you. Seems to me it was automatic, wasn't it?"

Rachel nodded but argued. "It shouldn't have been based just on our marks. I know that's how it has always been done but don't you think the valedictorian should be an all-around student? Someone who manages to have good grades and be socially acceptable? If they had used that sort of measurement to pick, it certainly wouldn't have been me, and you all might not have felt obliged to make that last week so completely dreadful."

Jake looked suitably miserable, and Rachel started to feel an opening within her heart that she might be able to forgive both him and the foolish youngster she had been.

"Anyway, fifteen years later is rather a long time to be holding a grudge, wouldn't you say?" she asked with as light a laugh as she could manage. Jake looked up at her with a trace of wonder on his face.

"Does that mean you might be able to stop holding it?"

"It's probably in my best interest," Rachel said with a laugh that required less force to make.

"Why, so I'll give you a bigger discount on the pier?" Jake asked.

Rachel suspected he was teasing, but she blushed anyway. "That wasn't what I meant, although I wouldn't refuse a discount," she added with a light laugh. "I was just thinking that it's not healthy to hold grudges. I'm not benefiting in any way from holding onto the hurt and anger."

"Ah, I see," Jake answered. "I was kind of hoping you might be open to trying to be friends."

"Why would you want to be friends with me?"

"Well," Jake drawled. "You're still the cutest little girl I've ever seen."

"Your niece might object to that statement," Rachel countered, although a sliver of pleasure countered her words.

Jake didn't bother arguing the topic, just looked around the room, staring at the doors she and Evelyn had painted. "Rachel, these turned out so well. You seem to have a real talent for refinishing," he complimented her.

"Now you're just sucking up," Rachel replied with laughter, pleased despite herself.

"I'm not, in this case. Refinishing can be really challenging, especially for someone not regularly doing these types of projects. I thought you said you had never done do-it-yourself work before."

"I didn't. My house in Chicago was brand new and was built by an experienced builder. There was nothing left undone when we moved in."

Jake nodded and gazed at her with elevated eyebrows. "Like I said." He grinned as her face heated. "So, in the spirit of trying to put the past behind us and be friends, can we hang these beauties for you, so you can get your kitchen back?"

Rachel wasn't sure if it was a good idea but since she had told him she was trying to stop holding the grudge, she supposed she ought to try to suit her words to action. She had to look down at herself to verify what she was wearing. Although she was sure the doors were completely dry, she didn't want to ruin any more items than she already had. If she was going to be living on a budget, she needed to conserve all her clothes as best she could. Besides, the shopping on the island consisted of beachwear and groceries.

"Sorry, my mind wandered for the briefest moment," she excused with an embarrassed laugh. "Sure, I would love some help with hanging them, as I'm afraid if I try doing it myself or even with Evelyn's help, we'll end up scratching off all the paint we put on."

"Well, it looks like you prepared the surface really well, so your paint has adhered very nicely, but there's no sense risking it," Jake agreed.

"Which tools do we need?" Rachel got to her feet and was heading toward the closet where she had stowed most of her tools. She was a little shy to let a professional carpenter see her small store of old tools, but Jake was heading out the door, much to her surprise.

He didn't go far, just to the back porch. He returned quickly with a small but clean and professional looking tool bag.

"I was optimistic," he said with a grin when she looked at his bag in surprise.

Before Rachel knew it, they were nearly finished putting her kitchen back together and had been chatting like old friends for a while despite the stilted beginning.

"So how did you get into writing historical fiction?"

"Why do you ask? Did you think I would be better at writing textbooks?" Rachel was actually teasing him back. She never would have thought she would see the day she would be that kind of comfortable with the handsome man.

"While I think you would be good at anything you tried, I hadn't ever pictured you as a writer, for some reason. Maybe because you seemed to always be so active as a kid. I thought it might be too still for you."

"Ah, I see," Rachel laughed. "And you might turn out to be right, although being an accountant probably requires as much or more stillness." She shrugged. "Nowadays, authors can even dictate or walk on a treadmill with a standing desk. I haven't gotten that sophisticated with my writing yet, but it takes less concentration and therefore less stillness than my old career."

Jake nodded and made some sort of noise as though to indicate he was listening even while he was attaching the last door.

"In answer to your question, I really wanted to try thrillers or mysteries. I think that's where the best money is. But I don't think my brain is devious enough. I've tried reading and deconstructing my favorite writers, and I just can't do it." Rachel laughed lightly and shrugged. "The historicals were easy to get started on, since that was my and Aunt Eileen's favorite books to read. We would read them together on vacations or each read them and then chat about them." She paused and made a sound of disgust. "My husband thought we were rotting our brains."

"Excuse me?" Jake sounded incredulous, making Rachel grin.

"Todd thought fiction, especially romantic fiction, was a waste of time and actually detracted from your intelligence rather than adding to it."

Jake was silent while he eyeballed the door he was hanging to make sure it was straight and even, but then he turned his attention fully toward Rachel.

"Did he not spend any time with you? Did he not realize how very smart you are?"

Rachel shrugged. "He might have been right. I'm not as smart as I was in school. Who knows?" she asked with half a shrug. "Maybe he was right, and it was the books I was reading."

"First of all, I'm of the school of thought that pretty much anything you read is going to make you smarter or at least stimulate your brain in some way," Jake began. "Second, I would think historical fiction, even of the romantic variety, would require more brain power because you have to visualize something that isn't familiar to you." Then he paused and laughed slightly. "I mean, I haven't read any of what you're talking about, but I do think the act of reading a book is just plain good exercise for your brain. Far better than watching tv, at the very least."

"Yeah, I agree with you, but having listened to that for several years, I'm a little sensitive about what I've chosen to try to do with my life."

"Well, even if there could be an argument made that reading a novel isn't productive for your mind, no one could successfully argue that writing one isn't. Just stringing together a sentence is a challenge for most people, let alone forming those sentences into paragraphs and chapters that make sense."

Rachel grinned, appreciating his supportive words, but then she lifted her shoulders helplessly. "We don't really know yet if my paragraphs and chapters make sense," she said with regret.

"Has anyone read them? Besides you, I mean?"

"Just Aunt Eileen."

"And what did she think?"

"She loved them," Rachel said firmly. "But she also really loved me."

"Of course, she did," Jake replied immediately. "But if she was such a reader of those kinds of books, she would probably be in the best position to tell you whether or not they were any good, wouldn't she?"

Rachel nodded thoughtfully. "I see your point, and I appreciate it. I feel like she might have been biased in her opinion, but I will try to keep what you've said in mind."

"Are you becoming insecure about your writing because of your late husband? Or is it something else? If no one else has read it, you don't actually have any reason to think it's no good."

Rachel laughed. "I do appreciate your logic, Jake, thank you. But I wasn't completely honest, or rather I didn't tell you the details. I've started submitting to agents and have so far only received rejections." When his face fell, she elaborated. "I did receive one request for a full manuscript after the agent had read my first three chapters, but then she rejected the full."

"That just means she wasn't the right one for you."

"Are you just being this nice because you think you need to be absolved of your past misdeeds?"

"You certainly are the suspicious sort, aren't you?" Jake laughed. "No, that's not why, although I would love to be absolved of the past. I went to school with you, remember? I was in your English class for four years. I remember some of your writing. You were really good, even as a kid. I can imagine that you'd be even better now."

Rachel stared at him, feeling tears prickle the back of her eyes. "That's the nicest thing you've ever said to me," she said.

"Well, that's not hard," Jake replied with a bashful nudge of his foot. "I didn't have anything nice to say to you back then."

To her surprise, Rachel laughed. "True, but still, you didn't have to say that now, so I really appreciate it. And you're right, you actually did hear some of the things I've written. Todd never did. So, I'm going to place more weight on your words than on his."

"Good," Jake declared with a nod, even though he seemed uncomfortable.

"What's wrong?" Rachel queried.

"Seems to me you've been rather hard done by with most people in your life, at least by any men in your life."

Rachel was struck into silence by his observation. He wasn't necessarily wrong, although there hadn't been all that many people in her life. But then she rallied.

"I'm learning to look at the brighter side of things," she explained slowly. "I'm accepting that Aunt Eileen truly loved me and did her very best for me. Even in her death, she is looking after me. If not for this house and the small inheritance she left, I would be in a tough spot right now." She cast her gaze out the window even as she looked into the past in her mind's eye. "And my childhood really was idyllic. My parents were awesome and raised me well. I really shouldn't have allowed myself to go into a tailspin for more than half of my life after their deaths."

"Well, you were thirteen. Anyone losing both their parents at once at that age would have trouble dealing with it."

Rachel nodded. "Ok, you're probably right. But now is new, and I have to make it better. I am done lamenting."

"That's a great attitude," Jake enthused, making Rachel laugh.

"It sounds good, but it's very difficult for me to rewire my entire thought process."

Jake nodded. "I can see that. It's like when I decided to come back to the island after bumming around for a few years. I had to rethink everything to go from being rather flighty to become responsible and start thinking about roots and plans and a future."

"Do you miss it?" Rachel asked softly.

Jake turned to meet her gaze, and Rachel's stomach dipped, but not in a bad way. It actually kind of reminded her of the first time she had seen him when she was thirteen. And didn't know what was in store for them. All she had known at the time was that he was the handsomest guy she had ever seen. He still was, which was rather disconcerting. And there was a great deal of hurt under the bridge. But she was ready to put that behind her. She didn't know if she could forge a friendship with someone who had been so associated with the pain she had experienced, but there was no rush to decide that. He was being nice, helping her finish this little project. Maybe she would hire him for the pier and finish up the house so she could fully move on with her life here. But there were definitely butterflies. Rachel suspected they were the butterflies of attraction. She hadn't felt them since college. It was a heady feeling. And the sparkle in his gaze made her suspect he might possibly be feeling them, too. But she was far from ready for that, so she took a step back and turned the subject.

"Wow, Jake, thank you so much, this looks fantastic."

"I didn't do that, you did. All I did was help you reassemble the pieces."

"I don't think I would have been able to do that so well on my own. You had been right about that. So, thank you for dropping in and kind of insisting. I have a tendency to try to refuse help."

"I might have noticed that," he said with a laugh. "I'm glad I was able to do it. But really, you did such a great job with the painting." He looked around the rest of the room. "It all ties in well together now."

Rachel laughed lightly. "Yeah, I am very curious about this room, to be honest. It was so out of sync with the rest of the house. Now it feels much more harmonious. The dark cupboards certainly brought the whole main floor down. Now it has a lighter and airy vibe. I like it."

"Do you think you're going to stay?" he asked with a trace of something she couldn't identify in his voice. Rachel wondered if he was hoping she would or wouldn't. It didn't matter.

"I hope to. I'm waiting to hear back from a possible job that I could do part time from here. It will keep the lights on and food on my table at least, and then I can concentrate on my writing for a little while and see where that goes."

"I'd love to hear more about it," Jake said glancing into the living room as though to hint that he'd like to be invited to sit again.

Rachel bit the inside of her cheek, uncertain if she wanted to spend any more time with him. Then she glanced at the coffee pot.

"Do you need to get to your jobsite? Or could I offer you a cup of coffee or something? It's the least I can do after you've helped me so much."

"I didn't really do anything," Jake excused. "But I'd love a cup, thank you."

Rachel laughed and started the process. She felt like all thumbs with Jake watching her, so she gestured for him to wait for her in the front room.

"Go ahead and have a seat. I'll bring this in as soon as it's ready."

"I'd rather keep you company and help you carry anything."

Rachel's face heated, and she nearly spilled the water she was pouring into the coffee maker. Was he flirting with her? What was she supposed to do with that? Then other worries crossed her mind. She didn't have anything like cookies or pastries that she could offer him. She ought to be more of a homemaker like

Evelyn, she thought with despair as she tried to remember the contents of the fridge.

"I'm sorry, I don't have anything much to offer along with the coffee, as I emptied out my kitchen before I started on the cupboards."

"Don't worry about it," Jake countered promptly. "I try to avoid sweets anyway. Since I hit thirty, every cookie likes to stick around."

"Even with being a carpenter?"

Jake shrugged. "I used to eat a lot of cookies," he said with a laugh.

Rachel busied herself with cream and sugar for the coffee, not meeting his eyes.

"You never answered me about whether or not you miss your nomadic life." She kept herself facing the counter, uncomfortable with the rather personal question but quite curious about the answer. She almost squirmed as the silence lengthened between them. When he sighed, she glanced at him over her shoulder, cringing at the thought that she had made him uncomfortable. Despite their past, she certainly hadn't wished for revenge.

"Sorry, Rach," he began, running a hand through his hair. "I'm not dithering on purpose. I'm just not sure how to answer your question."

"You don't have to if you don't want to."

"No, it's just that no one has asked me that before. And I have to decide how I actually feel."

Rachel laughed. "I can totally relate to that sentiment." She busied herself again with the coffee. "Wait until we're sitting with our mugs, and we can discuss it."

Jake nodded, looking pleased with her offer.

Once they were settled, Rachel leaned toward him slightly with her eyebrows lifted in inquiry, making him laugh.

"Ok, if you don't actually know how you feel, then just tell me about it. Where did you go first? What made you leave? How did you get there?"

Jake appeared uncomfortable still, but he started to talk after shifting his gaze to the window in front of them.

"I left just a couple weeks after graduation. I went first to Long Island. It wasn't too hard to get there, just a few hours north. I stayed with my uncle and aunt who lived there. I mostly just hung out in a park near their house. I learned how to skateboard that summer," he trailed off.

"You don't strike me as the skater boy type," Rachel commented, making him smile a little.

"Yeah, I'm not. But it was fun. There wasn't really much surfing in Long Island, the port was too busy, I guess. But it was a similar skill."

Rachel nodded, watching him even while taking a sip of her coffee. She wondered why he was having such a hard time telling her his story. Finally, he sighed.

"I left the island because it felt empty here without you."

Rachel blinked and stared at him with a frown gathering on her forehead.

"What do you mean?"

"I mean that I was two years older than you. At our graduation, I was already nineteen. Not the most mature nineteen-year-old you'd ever met but already maturing to some extent. I saw your face that night. I knew what we had done, or at least understood to a certain extent that we had hurt you."

Rachel swallowed. She didn't bother to point out that she had been devastated. This wasn't about her at the moment. She wasn't going to argue about the extent of her injury when it was evident that he was already aware, even back then.

"How does that tie in with your leaving?"

"Guilt, I suppose. I had actually foolishly hoped that once we graduated and maybe got away from our friends that you and I could find our way to one another."

A puff of air escaped Rachel that might have been a little laugh, but she didn't say anything.

"I know, kinda stupid. But, as I said, I was only mature enough to realize we had hurt you pretty bad, not mature enough not to believe in wishes."

Rachel's mouth opened and closed without anything coming out in between. Jake continued.

"Anyway, I couldn't stay here. Guilt wasn't a good companion, and neither were my friends. I didn't want to see any of them since I knew what we had done and that I had started it years before. So, I hung out in Long Island until my uncle's wife's murmuring got too loud to ignore. After that, I just bounced around from place to place. First, I wanted to escape the winter, so I headed to Florida. Then I heard California was the place to be, so I spent almost a year there between a couple cities. After that, I went to Europe for a while."

"Europe," Rachel exclaimed. "Was that as wonderful as I've always imagined?"

Jake lifted a shoulder and glanced toward her. "Sort of. I would like to go back now that I'm a bit more settled and see how I feel about it. I'm sure you would love it."

Rachel smiled, wondering what exactly he meant by that but allowing him to continue his story.

"I would find work in coffee shops or restaurants, waiting tables here and there, basically just working enough to eat."

"What did you do with your time, then?"

"I hiked, and travelled, and worked out," he shrugged. "It was pretty aimless." His chuckle was dry. "In my defense, though, I did have to work a fair bit to keep myself housed and fed. They weren't big tippers, and the pay wasn't great."

"Did you enjoy it, at least?"

"Most of the time," he nodded.

"What brought you back stateside?"

"I missed my family. I came for a holiday and just never went back."

Rachel frowned. "How long were you gone?"

"Four years."

"Wow."

"Yeah," he nodded. "Some people actually just thought I was away at school."

Rachel laughed a little. "It was probably quite educational, so they're not completely wrong."

Jake nodded.

"And then what? How did you get into construction if you were a waiter up until then?"

"Another one of my uncles insisted. He said I was being flabby and useless, and I might as well help him out."

Rachel grinned. "You must have loved that."

"Actually, I did. I needed someone to just take charge for a minute and call me out on being a bum. I worked for him for several years. He helped me get into trade school as his apprentice. When he decided to retire, he wanted me to just take over his business, but by then my sister was pregnant and I wanted to be here to help her out."

"She didn't want to join you wherever you were?"

"Our parents were also here at the time, so this was the better fit for all of us. And it was a good move for the island, too, as there were no construction companies permanently here. With the size of the island, I could be even busier than I am if I wanted to be. But I still want to have some flexibility. I want to be at every single one of my niece's little events. And I like to travel a little. It's just a week or two at a time now rather than years."

"That sounds quite lovely," Rachel remarked.

"Which part?" Jake asked with a laugh. "Travelling or my niece?"

"All of it. It sounds like you found a good balance for yourself. It takes many people even longer than it took you."

"Do you mean you?" he asked gently.

Rachel shrugged but nodded. "Yeah. It took losing everything to make me realize there was no balance in my life."

"But you travelled at least a little bit, didn't you?"

"A little. Mostly weekend meet ups with my aunt. But they were fantastic. I lived for those. But that's not really indicative of a healthy balance when you're living for a weekend getaway. That's why I'm hoping to be able to stay on here and just work part time. I don't know what else I'll do. I've never had hobbies before. But I'm looking forward to finding some."

Jake grinned. "Too bad you don't have nieces or nephews. You would then be able to discover that you don't hate having your fingernails painted by a three-year-old and that imaginary tea is the best kind."

Rachel stared at him trying to imagine the big handsome man fitting himself into a miniature chair to please his sister's small child. She couldn't picture her high school tormentor doing such a thing, but she could actually see this man doing so. She smiled.

"I do wish I'd had siblings who could now provide me with nieces and nephews, but it's a little late for that. Now I'm making friends with people who have kids, so maybe I'll be able to have the same experience."

"Oh yeah, who have you been hanging out with?"

"Well, Evelyn for one."

"They don't have kids."

"Not yet, but they will. And I'll have a front row seat for it. I can't wait. I'm getting nearly as excited about that as Evie." Rachel laughed. "Ok, maybe that's an exaggeration, but I can't wait for them to figure out what they're doing."

"I'm glad you're starting to get more settled."

Rachel nodded. "I'm starting to figure out that maybe my life wasn't so blighted after all," she added with a gentle smile. "So, tell me about this pier. When will you have room in your schedule, do you think?"

Chapter Twenty-Two

J ake couldn't believe he had spent half the day with Rachel just talking and drinking coffee. He was nearly bursting from all the coffee, so he supposed he could believe that. He laughed to himself as he finally arrived at his jobsite to check on his crew.

The workers had managed just fine without him. He had known they would, of course, but it was good to have the reassurance. Especially since he was going to try to do Rachel's work himself. He would need help from his guys for some of it, but the rest he wanted to take on himself. For many reasons, not the least of which he still felt like he owed her. But he also wanted all the excuses he could muster to be around her.

She still didn't seem to realize she was the prettiest girl he had ever seen, even though he'd told her so. She thought he meant when she was little. While she had been pretty cute even as a thirteen-year-old, which just thinking that made him feel a bit like a perv, but she had turned out to be a gorgeous woman. Maybe a little too thin, but that was probably just because of her recent circumstances. She didn't strike him as the sort who would starve herself.

Although, what did he really know?

He hoped he wasn't going to make a fool of himself. But he didn't really care if he did. If he was man enough to wear a tutu with his niece, he could weather rejection from a beautiful woman. And no one would blame her for rejecting him. But those same no ones wouldn't blame him for at least trying. She was beautiful, intelligent, articulate, and wanted to stay on the island. She even seemed open to the idea of forgiving him for his mistreatment of her when they were young. That was the most amazing part.

Jake didn't deserve her forgiveness, but he wouldn't say no if she was offering it. He was also hoping she would consider offering him her friendship. But he would take what he could get for the time being. And that was fixing up the outside of her house. Not the actual house, just the land in front and into the water.

It was going to be a massive job. He couldn't wait to get started.

In hindsight, it was odd that her aunt had let it get so bad. Theirs was the only house on the shore that had a rundown pier. It made the place look neglected. Maybe it had already started to deteriorate when Eileen had found out she was sick, and she just didn't have it in her to pursue the major project. Hadn't Rachel mentioned all the other maintenance type projects she was doing in the house? It would seem Eileen had let several things go in recent times. Just the pier was more evident from the outside. It would start being a problem soon if Rachel didn't get on it.

He would be basically doing the job at cost for her. But he didn't care. He would do it completely for free, out of his own pocket, if it meant he could spend time with her.

Jake threw himself into finishing the deck his crew was working on as he worked through his thoughts.

Was he just hanging on to a memory or old guilt? That had been Rachel's question when she told him she had tried to look up her type of project and felt he had wildly underpriced her quote. He didn't tell her how off she had been in her calculations. He wouldn't be making a cent. But he couldn't make money off her. And he didn't think it was just his guilt.

Ok well, maybe not taking any profit was just his guilt. But if he could do that for her, why not do it? If fixing up her house and not spending her savings would set Rachel up for a better life, even if she decided she didn't want him in it, then he owed her that at the very least. And if he could live a little lighter, thinking he had made things even a little better for her, he would take it and carry on his own way.

Having cleared the air between them, it seemed they could at least coexist on the island without having to fear running into one another. Because he had worried about that when he'd first moved back to the island until his quietly asking around had revealed that Rachel had never been seen back since graduation.

She was thorough when she did things, he'd give her that, even keeping a grudge alive for fifteen years. Not that he could blame her. He wouldn't want to return to the scene of his pain either. He wouldn't have come back to the island himself if not for his family needing him.

He was just a little surprised she hadn't returned to help Eileen in her last days. Perhaps she wasn't the warm, sweet woman he wanted to think her if she could leave her only relative to die alone. He would wait and see. He would try to be reasonable about Rachel Whitney, but it would be a challenge considering the pedestal he had put her on for more than fifteen years. It was unlikely that she would live up to it.

Whichever way this went, though, maybe now he would be able to truly settle down. The way he'd treated her in school had always eaten away at the back of his mind. Or rather the guilt had. It had made it impossible for him to succeed in any relationship with women. Now that he'd seemingly made peace with Rachel, maybe he could finally find someone to build a future with.

What if that someone was Rachel?

The thought followed him around all day and into the night, interfering with his ability to sleep, and it kept right on nipping at his heels when he finally threw back the covers and went for a long run hoping to outrun it.

While it was true that she was a beautiful, intelligent woman, he wasn't sure if their past would allow for a healthy dynamic. And then there was her leaving her aunt like that. Family was the most important thing to Jake. He would never be able to abandon them the way Rachel had. Even though essentially it was Jake's fault, he wasn't sure if it was something he could live with.

Not that she was likely to be giving him the chance to see where a relationship between them could go.

She had been a pleasant companion for several hours, but she hadn't really given much indication that she was looking for anything other than friendship. And even that was perhaps putting an optimistic spin on her feelings.

She had been pleasant and polite. Thanking him for helping her with her project. And she did hire him for the pier at the bargain basement price he had offered her. Of course, she would accept that offer. He had made it impossible to refuse.

There had been a time or two throughout the morning that Jake had thought that her eyes might be admiring him, and she had seemed relaxed enough in his company, but she certainly hadn't put out any of the come-hither vibes he was used to receiving from women.

Jake sighed, which interfered with his breath as he was running, and he had to slow his pace. Since he was going to be working at her house for a couple weeks or more, he would be forced to be in her company. He would see for himself what sort of person she was. And also get to see whether she would even consider a relationship with him.

He would have to be satisfied with a wait-and-see attitude. It wasn't his favorite situation, but there was nothing else to do about it. Where Rachel was concerned, he had already been waiting almost two decades, a few more weeks wouldn't harm him.

Chapter Twenty-Three

What had she been thinking?

Rachel paced in front of her computer. She should be writing, but she couldn't get her thoughts to focus. She definitely couldn't do any accounting work with her mind such a jumble. And every crack and crevice of her house was spotless and dust free.

It had been a week since she and Jake had hung her cupboard doors. Her kitchen was restored to more than its former glory. The entire house shone.

Even the main floor bathroom. She had taken Evelyn's advice and used baking soda on the grout. It had taken a great deal of elbow grease, but she'd had a frustration or two to work out, so it had been a win-win. The grout might be cleaner than it had been originally at this point. The thought actually amused her. But it was true. It was spotless. She had then sealed it to make sure it stayed that way, at least for a while. Eventually she might decide to redo that bathroom anyway, but baking soda certainly fit better into her budget than an entire reconstruction.

In the last week she had also heard back from Evelyn's author friend. That had been a thrill. The woman had been very kind about her opening chapters and had asked to read the rest of the story. She had written to Rachel to say that if the rest of the book lived up to its opening, there was a good chance she had a bestseller on her hands. She had been full of advice for Rachel, which had filled her head and made it spin.

Evelyn, of course, had been ecstatic.

"I knew it! I knew you had to be an awesome writer," she had declared when Rachel told her what Catherine Stewart had said. "But I don't have any actual knowledge or experience, so I'm thrilled she was able to tell you that."

"Thank you so much for connecting us." Rachel hugged her friend.

"What are you going to do next?" Evelyn asked.

Rachel raised her eyebrows. "Next with what? The house? Or my writing? Or work? Or more existentially – life?"

Evelyn laughed. "All of the above?"

Rachel joined her in laughing but then sighed and flopped down on the couch Evelyn was already sitting on.

"I don't know. I'm trying to keep writing while I wait for Catherine's verdict on the rest of my story. She promised to be fast because she was anxious to see how it develops, but she also wants to give me suggestions on where to tighten up the storyline. As an aside, I'm not one hundred percent sure what that exactly means, so I'm hoping she goes into detail. Although I should just be grateful."

"Well, it's not much help if it isn't clear, so I don't think it sounds like a lack of gratitude."

"Evelyn, you are the best, thank you for saying that." Rachel paused for a moment before gasping. "I forgot to tell you! I also finally heard back from that company I hoped to do some accounting for. And they want me."

"Of course they do, they'd be fools not to." Ever loyal, Evelyn always had supportive things to say.

Rachel laughed. "It's only a temporary contract for now while we work out the details of what exactly they'll need from me, but I'm feeling a little more confident about my abilities in that sphere, and I'm excited to get back into it."

Evelyn didn't have anything to add, just nodding eagerly as Rachel spoke, so she carried on.

"Anyhow, life in general seems to really be coming together for me in a way that makes me nervous."

Evelyn stared at her with surprise. "What's that supposed to mean?"

"Life hasn't really gone my way, you know? Like in big, fundamental ways. I have been happy, of course. Humans are amazingly resilient. Even when things are bad, we can still be happy. But I lost my parents when I was thirteen. I was tormented through school. I married someone who didn't turn out to be a true partner, and then I lost everything we had built when he was killed. And my only living relative died alone in a hospice bed because I was too much of a wimp to rock the boat in my unhappy marriage."

Evelyn's sympathetic gaze was filling with tears, and Rachel hurried to reassure her. She waved her hands in front of her as though to brush away what she had already said. "Don't look at all that. That's the past. But that's why I am having a hard time trusting the present. For more than half my life, when things look like they're settling down nicely, that turns out to be a lie. So, I'm worried this will all turn out to be quicksand under my feet."

"What all of this are you talking about specifically?"

"My new friendships, my new job, my house, my writing."

"Oh, so everything," Evelyn said with a laugh before sobering and grasping her friend's hand. "I for one am not going anywhere. I think you're great, and I won't easily be dissuaded from that opinion. There's no reason why your new job should disappear. And unless the worst hurricane in history were to sweep through, your house should be fine for at least another few decades. Your updates here and there made a surprising difference."

"I had help from a good friend," Rachel replied, squeezing Evelyn's hand in return.

"As for your writing, if Catherine thought you have potential, then you certainly do. If you're determined and as smart as I think you are, even if she thinks your book needs work, you can do the work."

"You're right, thank you."

"But something tells me it's really something else that's bothering you," Evelyn pointed out. "Perhaps the eye candy out in the surf working on your pier?"

Rachel's cheeks heated. "I don't know what you're talking about," she said with a laugh.

Evelyn narrowed her eyes at her. "Yes, you do, you just don't feel comfortable talking about it yet."

Rachel sighed as she remembered the conversation with her friend. And Evelyn really was her friend. While Angela and Tina were great, and Rachel enjoyed spending time with them and was more and more thinking of them as friends, they were more preoccupied with their own lives and weren't as quick as Evelyn to incorporate Rachel into their daily living. Of course, it was easier for Evelyn as she was right next door, and she was currently very available. Only time would tell if it would continue once she became preoccupied with her own children once they started arriving. But Rachel assured herself, by then she would have herself set up with a comfortable, flexible schedule that would allow her to be adaptable to her friend's needs so Rachel could be the doting aunt she was determined to be.

But that still left the matter of Jake. The thing she hadn't wanted to admit to Evelyn earlier in the week. As Evelyn had said, he was certainly eye candy. But he was also thoughtful, intelligent, and a shockingly good listener. When she couldn't keep herself away from his side, she found herself babbling to him far more than she had ever done in her life with anyone else.

Favorite foods, movies, music, books, they seemed to agree or be able to comfortably disagree on nearly every topic they had yet settled upon. And the way he spoke about his little niece. Rachel felt as though she knew the child already even though they had yet to meet. Between Jake showing her pictures and all his stories, Rachel was half in love with the little girl without having laid eyes on her in real life. Jake's attachment to the child was obvious and contagious.

And so, Rachel found herself pacing in her cozy little office trying to be productive while avoiding the beach, where she really wanted to be.

Todd had only been dead for a little over three months. How could she be so disloyal as to have a crush on someone else so soon? But was it really a crush? And was it really all that soon? She had known Jake since she was thirteen. But she was too old for crushes. And if it was only lingering complicated feelings from her childhood, then she ought to see a therapist rather than allow it to affect her life.

Out on the beach, Jake was dragging a long piece of something. Even while squinting, she couldn't be certain what it was. But he was working alone, and it looked awkward. With a sigh, Rachel gave up the solitary mutterings that were getting her nowhere, threw on a sweatshirt and sneakers, and ran down to offer him a hand.

"Good morning," he called out to her, seeming delighted to see her.

She blushed with matching delight even as she admonished herself not to be ridiculous.

"No helpers today?" she asked as she grabbed the end.

"Everyone is needed on my other sites today," he said, confirming to Rachel that he had indeed put himself out for her property.

"Sites as in plural?" she queried, making him laugh.

"Yeah," he drawled. "We're trying to get as much done as possible through the winter so that we can all take August off. Maybe even July."

"What's happening then?"

"Do you mean besides being too hot for physical labor?" Jake asked with a grin that she matched. "Mostly we all just want to have vacations and rest. Everyone is willing to work harder and longer now with that in mind."

"That's cool. Especially for anyone with kids, I suppose. They can be home or go on vacations, while their kids are off school."

Jake nodded. "Whatever happens, I intend to take as much of the summer off as possible, even if I have to just stop by my sites from time to time if the guys are working."

"They might not appreciate that," she pointed out.

"Another reason why my doing this job mostly by myself is so good. It's getting them used to my not being on hand all the time."

Since Rachel wasn't completely comfortable with her newfound comprehension that he had taken this job on himself as a favor, she didn't delve into that topic.

"Are you trying to cut back more permanently? Or just for the summer?"

Jake didn't answer her question right away, concentrating on attaching the rebar they were holding.

"That is still to be determined," he finally answered her. "I've been pretty focused on building up my business for several years now. But I guess I'm like you, looking for a little more work-life balance as they say."

Rachel nodded although he wasn't looking at her at the moment.

"What are you hoping to do with your time?"

"I want to spend more time with my niece, for one thing. She isn't going to be this young and cute forever. Soon she probably isn't even going to want to play tea party with me anymore."

Rachel laughed at the mental picture that conjured for her. "I'm surprised, given how much you so obviously adore her, that you haven't had any of your own."

"Need a wife for that," he grunted. "Science has come a long way, but there's only so much a man can do on his own."

"Are you looking for one?" Rachel asked, regretting the question as soon as it was out of her mouth.

Jake turned and scoured her with his searching glance. "Are you volunteering?" he asked with a grin and a suggestive wiggle of his eyebrows.

"I've just gotten out of a less than ideal situation. I'm not sure if I'll ever be looking to get leg shackled again."

"Leg shackled?" Jake asked with humor sounding in his voice. "What's that supposed to mean?"

Even though his concentration was still centered on the work he was doing, a blush flooded Rachel from head to toe. "Sorry, my vocabulary is sometimes stuck in the early nineteenth century."

"Is that how your characters would refer to marriage?" he asked, evidently interested despite his focus on his task.

Rachel nodded. "Yeah. Especially a duke who doesn't really want a wife but feels duty bound to produce an heir."

Jake laughed. "I do hope you're going to help him get over that attitude."

"Of course."

"Why don't you get comfortable and tell me about it?" he invited. "Unless you need to get back to your work."

"I feel bad to leave you to do all this by yourself. I ought to be helping you."

"Is that what brought you down here? Guilt?"

"It's a powerful motivator that I'm very familiar with," Rachel answered, scuffing the sand with her toe.

"Rachel," Jake began, finally able to put down his tools and run a hand through his hair. "I would really like us to be friends but only because we both think the other is worth our time, not because of something so ugly as a guilty conscience. You have absolutely nothing to feel guilty over when it comes to me. And I've told you I'm sorry for the past, and you appear to have accepted my apology. You haven't actually said whether or not you have forgiven me, but that isn't the current point. I don't want you to be here out of guilt. Even out of a sense of obligation because I'm working alone. I chose that. And I'm a big boy. I won't lift anything I don't have full confidence I can handle on my own. Now if you'd like to keep me company, I would appreciate that, but I don't need an assistant for this task, and I don't want a grudging companion."

It was the longest stretch of words he'd ever addressed to her, and he said it in such a serious tone of voice that Rachel felt her eyes widening as he spoke. Finally, when he stopped and just stared at her silently as though daring her to respond, she offered him a tentative smile.

"Well, if you're sure you don't actually need me to pass you stuff, I'll go get a chair."

"So, you don't mind staying?" He sounded so eager Rachel couldn't have left even if she had wanted to.

She lifted one shoulder. "I'm pretty much done with almost everything in the house, and I had just finished my minimum word count for the day when I saw you, so I'm pretty much free."

"That sounded fairly vague," Jake countered with a chuckle. "But I'm going to take it at face value and accept your company. And if you would actually not mind handing me stuff, you could sit on my toolbox and pass me things from time to time."

Without further ado, Rachel found herself perched quite comfortably on his low toolbox, telling him all about the adventures of the hero and heroine in the manuscript she was halfway through.

And just like that, before she knew it, half a day had passed in Jake's company, and she hadn't laughed so much in years. It was the strangest sensation feeling so comfortable in someone's presence. Especially when she had harbored such animosity for that someone for so long. Rachel had so dreaded encountering Jake that she had never returned to the island while her aunt was alive. And now she was sitting here in the sun, on the beach, laughing and enjoying the man's company. She was a fool. And the most overwhelming wave of guilt swamped her, and she stood abruptly.

"I just remembered something," she said. "I have to go." And without any further explanation or even a farewell, Rachel hurried away toward the house, hoping he wouldn't see or hear as she fell apart inside.

The only relief she could feel was the fact that she had managed to get inside with the doors locked and even drew the curtains and blinds closed before she broke down completely. With her fist stuffed over her mouth she was even able to stifle the sobs and wails that erupted from her with irregular frequency. Nearly blinded, Rachel made her way upstairs and slumped in front of the door she had still been unable to open.

"Aunt Eileen," Rachel sobbed out softly. "Why can't you be here to absolve me of all this guilt? Why did I stay away? Why didn't you tell me you were sick? Why did you allow me to be such an idiot?"

Finally, drained and drawn, Rachel made her way to her own room and threw herself onto her bed, finally fading into restless sleep after the storm had lightened slightly.

For three days she alternated between flailing herself with reproachful thoughts, weeping, and sleeping. She ignored the frequent knocking on the door. She just didn't have it in her to face Evelyn's cheerful optimism. If Evie knew the extent of Rachel's betrayal of Eileen, even she couldn't cheer her way out of rejecting Rachel as her friend. Once or twice, Rachel thought she heard Jake calling her name, but that only made her burrow deeper under the covers and cry a little more. She couldn't face any of them.

With a sigh, on the fourth day, Rachel took herself to task. Eileen was not the sort to hold grudges. That was all Rachel's purview – not something to be proud of but also not something her aunt could ever be accused of. Finally, parched and cried out, Rachel forced her nearly atrophied limbs to help her climb out of the bed. She knew she had to accept and face her new reality. And part of that was to make peace with and accept the fact that her dearly beloved aunt was no longer with her.

Rachel couldn't even meet her own gaze in the mirror, so disgusted was she with herself, both for all her past actions and for the last three days of wallowing in misery. Rachel padded down the hallway and stood in front of her aunt's bedroom doorway. The only room in the house she hadn't yet entered since taking possession of the house and settling in like she owned the place.

Well, she did own the place, she thought with the first glimmer of a smile that she'd felt since that morning at the pier with Jake. Her aunt had been looking after her even in her death.

Rachel took a deep breath and held it as her hand hovered over the doorknob. She pulled back her shoulders as well as she could in the weakened state of starving and crying for three days and resolutely turned the knob to step into the room.

It was as though Eileen had just left. Rachel could still smell her aunt's favorite perfume on the still air. She quickly stepped inside and shut the door, not wanting to lose that beloved memory. Rather than feeling like she was violating her aunt's privacy, she now felt as though Eileen were hugging her close like she always had.

Rachel looked around the familiar space, relieved that she hadn't yet done anything in that room. She really needed the familiarity provided by the unchanged room. Not that she had altered the rest of the house so very much, but in her despair, what little she had done felt like a violation of her aunt's memory.

Standing over the dresser strewn with Eileen's favorite little items like her perfume, hair clips, earrings, and paperbacks, Rachel avoided her reflection, horrified to see the ravages of her three-day grief binge. Her gazed snagged on an envelope that was sticking out from a stack of books. Was that her name on it?

With trembling hands, Rachel pulled it toward her. Could she bear to read whatever might be inside?

My darling Rachel,

I know you're finding this after my death as I haven't told you how sick I am. I'm sorry for that. I should have told you long ago, but I kept hoping I would be able to beat it and I just didn't want anything negative to touch our times together. You should understand this as I know you have kept things to yourself that you ought to have told me. I'm not saying that to reproach you, I just hope you'll understand why I didn't tell you. Then, when I finally realized it was too late, I didn't want to waste the little bit of time I had left with you trying to accept my impending death.

Anyway, let's put that aside for now. I know my time is almost up and there are things I have to tell you.

My darling girl, you need to find your path. I know you aren't on the right path for you. You could be so happy and have a marvelous life. Please find it. I am proof that life is much too short to waste any of it.

I am leaving you whatever is left after my medical expenses. I hope it might help you find that path. But please don't feel any sentimental obligations to anything in this house, including the house itself. I know you will want to wallow in guilt when you find out I've died. Don't do it. And don't associate those feelings with this house. I have loved this house well for forty years. That is enough. I won't be here so don't feel that you're holding onto me by holding onto Sandpiper Cottage. I will always be in your heart because I know you've loved me. You must know and accept that I know that, my dear. Because that is my one worry. That you will feel that you should have known. I really didn't want you to know.

I know you have troubles of your own. I blame myself which is probably the worst of our family traits so I know you will struggle with similar feelings. I should have insisted that you come home for vacations no matter what you had sworn to yourself. But I didn't and here we are. Please don't let your husband take your inheritance or influence your decisions. Please choose joy.

Rachel could barely read the words through her tears and her aunt's declining handwriting. But she strained to keep going.

There is so much I should have told you. About my life and the choices I made. There isn't time now. But please know that I have always been happy. And the happiest years were the ones that had you in them. I was so filled with grief when my brother died, but your arrival on my doorstep was the bright spot that helped me get through. I know you can find your way to being the creature of joy I know you can be. Please know that I have loved you from the moment you came into the world until the moment I leave it. I have always supported your decisions and will continue to do so. But please, make sure you finish all the stories, both your own, and the make believe ones.

I will love you forever,

Aunt Eileen

Rachel thought she couldn't possibly have any more tears left in her body, but she had been wrong. However, these tears felt like a healing rather than the ravaging the last few days had been. Eileen might not have known fully why Rachel stayed away from home for so long, but she had forgiven her.

Forgiveness. What a strange word, Rachel thought as she sat on the floor with her head leaned back onto Eileen's bed. Rachel hadn't realized she had so needed her aunt's forgiveness, but Eileen had known and ensured she provided it, even as she lay dying. Rachel bit her knuckle to control her sobbing. Eileen wanted her to choose joy, and that was what she was going to do.

Glancing around the room, Rachel accepted that it would remain as it was for as long as necessary. It was in fine shape; Rachel couldn't see any cracks from where she sat. There was dust, of course, but even that Rachel didn't want to disturb for now. Someday. As Eileen had said, she would be in Rachel's heart, not in her house. But still, Rachel couldn't bear to make any changes just yet. Except for the needed changes within herself. That started right now.

With a decisive nod, Rachel got slowly to her feet. She might be feeling decisive, but she was also weak from having done nothing but cry and sleep for several days. She wasn't sure which should be her first stop – the shower or the kitchen – but she slowly found herself washed, with a towel around her long wet hair, sitting in the front room with a piece of toast in her hand, looking out over the dune to the pier that was taking shape in her own little personal piece of Atlantic Ocean shoreline.

Rachel took her time with that one piece of toast not wanting her stomach to revolt after what she had put it through that week. But when she had licked the peanut butter off her fingers and acknowledged that the toast seemed ready to stay where it was, Rachel finally reached for the phone she had ignored while she had wallowed.

As she had suspected, the notifications were overflowing. Texts and phone calls from Evelyn, Angela, and Jake. Even the more prickly Tina had expressed some concern for her. Rachel frowned. What day was it? Had she missed girls' night? She didn't think so but couldn't be sure. She sucked in a breath. There was the long-awaited email from Catherine Stewart, the best-selling author who was critiquing her story. The toast in her stomach rolled over but settled back down. Truly, after the week she'd had, it didn't matter what the author said. Even if she had hated every word Rachel wrote, that wouldn't break her. So, she clicked to read the author's message.

Hello Rachel,

Thank you for sharing your book with me. I was surprised to hear you say this is your first completed manuscript as it is remarkably well developed, even for a seasoned writer, let alone a rookie.

Rachel squealed with delight. She hadn't expected such high praise. If her legs weren't still weak, she would dance around the room. Aunt Eileen wished her joy, and it seemed she was going to find it after all. She returned to finish reading the message.

I would like to invite you to join a small group of local authors. I know you're not exactly local, but it would only take you about an hour to reach us. We meet in person once each month and online the rest of the time for the very reason of commute times, besides everyone's deadlines. But I think you'd be a good fit to join our little group. We have a lot of fun together and get some work done. Anyway, whatever you decide, I'd love to chat either over a cup of coffee or on the phone. I have a few suggestions about your story as well as your path to publication.

Hope to hear from you,

Catherine

Rachel squealed again. Catherine had included her phone number. Rachel promised herself that she would text her after she had responded to everyone else's messages. Who should she tackle first?

Evelyn. She could text Angela and Tina and arrange to meet them some evening, in fact, it was about time that she host girls' night, but Rachel's neighbor needed more than a text message. The poor woman had been calling and knocking for days. Rachel ought to face her in person. With a sigh that was only a little bit of resignation but also disappointment in herself combined with happiness that she actually had a friend who would call her to account for her behavior, Rachel went to put on some clothes for her encounter with Evelyn.

Chapter Twenty-Four

"Rachel? Rachel, I know you have to be in there. I'm going to break this door down if you don't open it in the next thirty seconds."

Rachel paused in the act of brushing her hair. That was Jake's voice. She didn't know if she was ready to face him just yet. But she couldn't allow him to break down her door. One last glance in the mirror assured her that she still looked like she had been sobbing for days, but at least her hair was neatly arranged, and she didn't have encrusted snots anywhere. This time her sigh was almost of relief. She would get it all over with at once it would seem. For she had heard Evelyn's soft voice accompanying Jake's.

"Hello," Rachel said as she opened the door. Evelyn and Jake both burst into her kitchen. Jake stared at her, but Evelyn immediately started fussing.

"Oh, Rachel, you poor thing. Have you been sick? You look like you've been sick. Not to say that you look badly, of course, but I can tell that you've lost weight. I should have brought a casserole with me."

Rachel blinked and burst into giggles right before pulling her dear friend in for a fierce hug.

"Evelyn, you are the dearest thing. I'm sorry that I frightened you. I was sort of sick. Heart sick, let's say, and I just couldn't face anyone. But that was irresponsible of me, and I'm sorry."

"No, no, dear girl, nothing to say sorry for. Well, Jake might feel differently, but I don't think so. But we need to feed you for sure."

Rachel laughed again. "I just had a slice of toast. I haven't eaten for a few days, so I don't want to risk eating very much right away."

Evelyn clucked with dismay, but Rachel wasn't really paying attention. It was Jake's fierce frown that had captured her gaze. She frowned in return.

"What's wrong?" she asked. "Did something happen?"

He didn't answer her right away, merely glowering at her as though trying to decide how to answer or perhaps how to control his feelings.

"Do you make a habit of disappearing like that?" he finally asked in a controlled voice.

"No, I've never done so before."

"That's actually not true," he pointed out. "You left here fifteen years ago, never to return until you were forced to do so."

Rachel stared at him. He wasn't wrong. She hadn't noticed the pattern before, but he was right. In the past, she had shut off the thing that had hurt her in a similar way, leaving the island and never returning. She bit her lip, unsure what to say in response.

Jake nodded at her and said in a clipped tone, "I'm glad you aren't dead. I'll be down at the shore." And he turned on his heel and left as abruptly as he had arrived.

"He has been worried nearly sick about you," Evelyn commented. "I think he might have feelings for you. The warm type of feelings, not the angry ones that he's showing right now. He really thought you might be in here dying."

Rachel sighed, running a hand over her ponytail as though to smooth it out. "I felt like I was, but it was figurative, not literal. I was dealing with some intense feelings and didn't handle it in the best way, obviously." She reached out and grabbed Evelyn's hand. "Thank you for caring and for not giving up. If I really was physically unwell, I would have appreciated your getting Jake to break in the door."

"He actually wanted to do it a couple days ago. Maybe I should have let him. What if you had really been hurt or something?"

Guilt assailed Rachel. A familiar emotion. But this time for much different reasons.

"I've never had people to be worried about me before, to be honest. Only Aunt Eileen. I would never have disappeared without telling her. I should have realized there were people who cared enough to worry." Rachel paused, taking a deep breath to feel the sincerity of her next words. "I promise I won't let it happen again."

Evelyn grinned. "I'll hold you to that. Now tell me what I can do. Do you want to talk about it? Or do you want me to feed you? Or do you want to go for a walk?"

"Oh, Evelyn, you are too good to me. Let's go for a walk."

Evelyn nodded but then frowned. "Have you eaten enough to have the strength?"

Rachel laughed a little. "I think so, but I'll bring a granola bar in my pocket just in case."

Evelyn beamed and happily headed for the door.

By the time they returned from their long rambling, Rachel had eaten the packaged snack and they had picked a date for a girls' night where she would introduce Evelyn to Angela and Tina. It wasn't a firm plan as she still hadn't received confirmation from the other two, but Evelyn was excited at the prospect. She had even had some insights into Tina's more prickly demeanor.

"She must care about you since she texted you while you were incommunicado. As you said, it was only three days. That was a long time for me, but I don't think you were in that much touch with those two, so it wouldn't have been so long to them," Evelyn explained.

Rachel was surprised and touched by that point.

"Didn't you say she's divorced? That has a tendency to make women bitter sometimes. Give her time. Sounds to me like she's a little jealous of you despite your losses. And maybe she's feeling insecure about adding you into the dynamic with Angela. Angela sounds like a much more open and accepting person, from what you've said about her, maybe that makes Tina feel threatened somehow."

Rachel stared at her friend and neighbor. "How do you have these insights and I, who actually know them, don't?"

Evelyn laughed. "It's easy to see from the outside."

"Well, I hope you'll still have insights when you're on the inside. I can't wait for you to meet them. I've read about the idea of found families. That's what I want to make for myself. And you're a big part of that."

They were both a little embarrassed by Evelyn's teary reaction to Rachel's words. Thankfully they were interrupted by one of Rachel's usual wave acquaintances. Of course, Evelyn knew them well and quickly introduced Rachel. By the time they'd returned, Evelyn had introduced Rachel to most of the neighbors from their lane. It was an odd coincidence that everyone was out strolling the beach that afternoon.

Rachel was ready to move beyond the superficial in her new life on the Cape. Some of the neighbors were actually people she had interacted with as a teen, and she had to swallow her embarrassment over not visiting them when she'd first returned. Thankfully, everyone was as gracious as Evelyn if not as enthusiastic about the new acquaintance.

The best part, though, was that she had promised to accompany Evelyn to her next appointment with her fertility doctor. Evelyn had explained that Eric had finally noticed her distress over Rachel and had taken the time to talk to her about all her concerns, including the possibility of adoption.

"Well, I'm glad that something good came out of your worries," Rachel said with a chuckle.

"I guess I am, too. Eric was really positive about the possibility of adopting if this next round of IVF doesn't work. But he agreed with you that maybe we should do both. While I would love the experience of carrying my baby, my track record hasn't been great, and there's no guarantee that I'll get more chances, even if this next one takes. And we don't want only one child. So, he agreed we should try both. Will you come with me?"

"To the adoption agency?" Rachel was both honored and slightly horrified. "Shouldn't the dad be the one to go with you?"

Evelyn shrugged. "I'd kind of like to interview them, if you know what I mean. And decide which agency I want to go with. I can do all the legwork first and then bring Eric."

Rachel nodded. "I am thrilled that you would entrust me with such a task," she answered sincerely. "Thank you. You name the day and I'll be ready."

Rachel was putting down roots in her little community, and it felt amazing. But there was one more person she had to make peace with. As they got closer to their houses, she saw Jake hard at work on her pier. It had progressed significantly while she had been checked out.

"I'm going to take him a coffee and try to talk to him."

"That's a good idea," Evelyn agreed with a nod as they parted ways near their homes.

Rachel's hands were sweating from nerves as she poured the mugs of coffee. She had found some old insulated cups in the cupboard and hoped Jake would be willing to hear her out over a cup of coffee. But she was ready to accept it if he didn't want to see her. She wouldn't like it, but she accepted that it wasn't ok for her to check out like she had.

Wiping her hands down her pant legs one more time before grabbing the two cups and the small bag of cookies Evelyn had brought over, Rachel made her way down toward where Jake was working on her new pier.

She was pretty sure he knew she was coming as he had stiffened suddenly, and his movements were more stilted than usual. But he kept his back to her even as she drew near.

"Hello, Jake," Rachel called after clearing the lump that had formed in her throat.

After what felt like an eternity but was probably just a dramatic pause, Jake turned to look at her. She couldn't read his expression but while he didn't look as though he was going to ask her to leave him alone, he also didn't appear overjoyed at the sight of her.

Rachel wanted to run away but braced her backbone. "I brought a peace offering," she said, holding up the coffee cups. "Could you take a little break and talk for a few minutes?"

"You're actually going to volunteer words?" he asked, sarcasm weighing his words down and making tears scratch at the back of her eyes.

Rachel swallowed the sensation. He was entitled to some skepticism.

"I know, I didn't act in the most mature fashion," she began, but he interrupted her.

"I know you've got a lot going on with grieving and all that, but I was actually worried about you when you disappeared like that. It was more than immature, Rachel, it was hurtful. Cruel even. I didn't think you were like that. But maybe you are. I mean, you didn't even come home when your aunt was sick, so maybe that's how you deal with things." Rachel must have made some sort of sound of distress because he suddenly looked contrite, but he continued speaking and didn't take back his words. "I had been really enjoying your company and had started to hope that maybe we could get over our past and forge at least a friendship or maybe even something more, but if you can't use your words to at least say you need a time out, then I don't think I can contemplate that."

Rachel's lips twisted with sudden amusement over his wording, obviously gleaned from his time with his niece, but she quickly sobered over the content of his message. "I'm sorry, Jake. You are right to be angry with me."

"I'm not angry, Rachel, I'm hurt. I know you aren't obliged to be friends with me after what I did to you in school, but you implied your forgiveness. And as a fellow human, I do deserve a certain treatment."

"You're absolutely right, Jake. I'm fully in the wrong in this case. I did have my reasons, but I should never have allowed my emotions to so completely override common decency." For a moment Rachel felt helpless, as there was really no excusing what she had done. But she was determined to try. "Would you allow me to at least explain?"

"Of course," he replied promptly, finally reaching out to take one of the cups from her hand. "Do you want to go up to your porch or sit here on the sand?"

The fact that he was willing to sit down encouraged Rachel to think he was willing to give her some of his time. Her hands were still sweating despite the cold wind. Again, she wished for escape, but if she'd learned nothing else in life, she had definitely learned that running away wasn't going to solve a thing.

"Over there would be good," she gestured toward where his tools were stored, forming a break from the wind. Jake's long legs ate up the distance and he quickly sat and looked at her expectantly. Rachel felt awkward as she tried to sit gracefully despite her nervous energy.

"I really am sorry, Jake. In my defense, the only person who ever would have really cared that I was missing in the past is dead, so it didn't cross my mind that anyone would be worried about me." When he made to object, she carried on. "I know, the ringing of my phone and the pinging of texts and emails should have clued me in, but I really wasn't quite in my right mind. But I swear I've learned my lesson and won't make that mistake again." She sighed heavily. "If you haven't fully retracted your offer of friendship, I would truly love to accept. I cannot promise that I won't make other mistakes, but I swear to you that I won't do something like that again."

"Fair enough."

Rachel blinked. "What does that mean? Now you're the one not using your words," she teased.

"I mean, I accept your apology and promise. The offer still stands."

It wasn't said with a great deal of enthusiasm, but Rachel wasn't going to split hairs. "Do you care to hear my explanation? It isn't an attempt at excusing my behavior, but I would like to try to explain it. If I can. I'm not even completely sure what happened. Nothing like that has ever happened to me before."

Now he frowned in concern. "Something happened? What happened? I thought you said you weren't sick or hurt." His searching gaze scoured her as though searching for an injury. Rachel smiled a little and then sighed again.

"It wasn't an illness, at least not a physical one." She paused for a moment. "You know how you said that I didn't even come home when my aunt was sick?"

"I shouldn't have said that, Rach, I'm sorry, it was low."

"But you weren't wrong. And that's what struck me that afternoon when we'd had such a good time working together. I was suddenly swamped with the ridiculousness of my past behavior. I had allowed my childish hurt feelings and silly vow to keep me away from home for fifteen years. Who does that? And it was all for a grudge I had been holding against you." She said that forcefully as though she couldn't believe it herself. "But there I was enjoying your company as though we were the best of friends, as though it had never happened. Why couldn't I have gotten to that point while Eileen was still alive?"

"Oh Rachel," Jake murmured, reaching over to clasp one of her hands.

Rachel felt the warmth of his large hand enveloping her much smaller one all the way down to her toes. The toes that curled in her sneakers and caused inappropriate flutters in her tummy. Now was not the time to be getting fluttery over a handsome man, she admonished herself.

She lifted her shoulder and tried to smile. "So, I had a little meltdown. I didn't know she was sick, not that sick anyway. I would like to think that I would have come if I had known, but I'll never really know. I thought I had already grieved, but I guess I hadn't. The grief and the guilt all came pouring out of me. I cried and slept for three days, thinking I could never forgive myself. But then I talked myself back into at least a semblance of sense."

She took a shuddery breath. Even though she was feeling bolstered, it was still painful to relive the experience. "I have been having very mixed feelings about the house ever since I got here, as I'm sure you can imagine."

"Yeah, you even felt badly about painting the cupboards."

Rachel nodded. "And I couldn't even go into my aunt's room. I painted, cleaned, plastered, and touched up pretty much every other surface in the house, but I couldn't open Eileen's door. Until this morning. I went in there, and I could almost feel that she had just left, you know? It was comforting, not creepy. I could even smell her favorite perfume."

"That's great, Rachel."

"Yeah, but I haven't even gotten to the best part. She wrote me a letter." Rachel swallowed. "I'm not ready to talk about that in detail, but it has changed everything for me."

"In what way?"

"She forgives me. And she knew I loved her. And, of course, she loved me. And she doesn't expect me to keep Sandpiper Cottage."

"Oh." Jake sounded disappointed.

"But I want to keep it. Because I love it here and am making friends here," Rachel squeezed Jake's hand that she was still holding tightly. "She just didn't want me to feel obliged. Or to keep it as a shrine to her. I'm still not ready or interested in changing her room, but that acceptance has really altered my perspective and feelings on the matter."

"I can see that. I'm happy for you," Jake said before his mouth widened into a grin. "And very happy for me."

"Why's that?"

"Because the cutest girl on the island just said she wants to be my friend."

Rachel laughed with genuine delight.

"And maybe that cute girl might consider being more than my friend," Jake added as he leaned in toward her.

"She actually really might consider it," Rachel replied breathily as Jake's free hand came up to caress the side of her head and cheek.

"Would it be too forward of me to kiss you right now?"

Rachel stared deep into Jake's brilliant green gaze, gratified that he had asked and thrilled that he was actually waiting patiently for her response. Eileen had been right to invite her to return to Sandpiper Cottage and to instruct her to choose joy. Rachel smiled and closed the distance between them. She might not know what the future held, but she was certain it was going to be amazing. She had friends to accompany her on her journey, she had the potential for a fun and rewarding career ahead of her, and the hopes for a fulfilling romantic relationship by her side.

She chose joy. And it was going to be perfect.

The End

Want to follow Tina's tumultuous journey?

Read:

Shelter at Sugar Beach

**She's determined to avoid romance.
Life has other plans..."**

The *Cape Avalon* series are W. M. Andrews' first contemporary set stories. If you're interested in reading her Historical Romance fiction, visit the Historical Books page on her website at www.wendymayandrews.com to learn more.

Consider starting her latest series – *Northcott Kinship*

Intriguing Lord Adelaide

She's a wallflower debutante—and his best friend's sister. But one dance could change everything.

About the Author

I learned to read when I was four or five, listening to my mother read to me when I was lonely after my brother started school. Ever since, I've had my head buried in books. I love words – historical plaques, signs, the cereal box – but my first love has always been novels.

A little over ten years ago my husband dared me to write a book instead of always reading them. I didn't think I'd be able to do it, but to my surprise I love writing. Those early efforts eventually became my first published book – Tempting the Earl (published by Avalon Books in 2010). It has been a thrilling adventure as I learned to navigate the world of publishing.

I believe firmly that everyone deserves a happily ever after. I want my readers to be able to escape from the everyday for a little while and feel upbeat and refreshed when they get to the end of my books.

When not reading or writing, I can be found traipsing around my neighborhood or travelling the world with my favorite companion.

Stay in touch:

My Website - sign up for my newsletter

www.wendymayandrews.com

Facebook   Instagram   Twitter

Made in the USA
Las Vegas, NV
27 May 2023

72598055R00146